H U N G R Y

HUNGRY

Joanna Torrey

Crown Publishers, Inc. · New York

Published by Crown Publishers, Inc., 201 East 50th Street, New York, New York 10022.
Member of the Crown Publishing Group.

Random House, Inc. New York, Toronto, London, Sydney, Auckland
http://www.randomhouse.com/

CROWN and colophon are trademarks of Crown Publishers, Inc.

Printed in the United States of America

Design by Lynne Amft

Library of Congress Cataloging-in-Publication Data
Torrey, Joanna.
Hungry / Joanna Torrey.—1st. ed.
p.   cm.
1. Women—United States—Social life and customs—Fiction.
I. Title.
PS3570.0738H86   1998
813'.54—dc21   97-15058
CIP

ISBN 0-609-60121-0

10 9 8 7 6 5 4 3 2 1

First Edition

CONTENTS

ACKNOWLEDGMENTS

. . .

With thanks to my editor, Ann Patty, her assistant, Pat Sheehan, and my agent, Neeti Madan. I am indebted to all my friends, family, and teachers who have offered me their encouragement, support, humor, patience, comments, and innumerable reading hours over the years. My gratitude to the Corporation of Yaddo for the gift of an undistracted month. And a very special thanks to my sister, Carolyn, for her unfailing confidence in me.

HUNGRY

WHEN IT CAME TO SEX, SHE MISSED BILL. SOMETIMES EVEN when it came to mealtimes, although that was rare. Bill liked Greek diners and cuchifrito stands. He would stand on the sidewalk eating rolling dark waves of fried pork skin and pig ears out of a paper bag. For him, a table was a table, four battered legs and a chipped Formica top. A dish was a dish. Bill didn't know the difference between fine dining and eating to survive.

Bill built motorcycles. Mostly, he sat at the kitchen table before and after a meal tenderly rubbing small parts of vintage Harleys with a dirty black cloth. He boasted that he would write a cookbook filled with iron-skillet dishes for hungry bachelor men. He ate his grayish layered men's pies with his head down close to his plate, chewing with his mouth a little open, breathing hard, as if he had a cold. She could sometimes see a flat pancake of food inside his mouth. She couldn't imagine him in pink and golden restaurants.

She thought she loved Bill, but she saw life stretching before her with no beautiful dinners—bleak, plain. Bill had no ambition.

She worried that she had none herself. They would sit forever
eating cheap stews out of metal serving bowls along with the kind
of white bread that came in loaves so long they filled up the whole
bottom of the shopping cart; loaves you could pinch into a wad of
chemicals the size of your fingernail. No seven-grain Swiss health
bread. No cabernet sauvignons so rich they smelled like the inside
of a cathedral. Just brown quarts of beer. She would turn into the
kind of woman who cooked one-and-a-half fish sticks in the
toaster oven. She would always be a secretary, worrying about
subway tokens and where to buy her morning bagel. They would
get strange together. She would start saving tea bags in the fridge
to use again, would fold rolls and crackers from restaurants into
napkins so that her purse was always filled with crumbs. She, who
wanted to grow old sitting on a velvet banquette, her hand devel-
oping arthritis around a glass of wine.

When she left Bill, she decided to focus on food. She signed up
for courses with international cooking celebrities. Not so much to
learn how to cook, but to develop her palate. At a class in mideast-
ern cooking at an Upper East Side town house, the teacher wore a
burnt-orange caftan with sleeves that trailed occasionally through
the flour. They learned to make pigeon pie wrapped in cinnamon-
dusted phyllo dough that crumbled like ancient rare manuscripts
at the touch of teeth. Reclining on bright-red mirrored pillows,
holding her plate under her chin and making small sounds of pleasure along with her classmates, she felt for the first time like someone with taste.

On the top floor of Macy's she watched in the overhead view-
ing mirror as a famous French chef whisked flour and butter into
a velvety smooth roux. The black hairs on his magically swiveling
wrist were magnified and electrically male. "Beat, beat, you must

not stop beating," he said in his charming French accent. When he asked for a volunteer from the audience, she jumped to her feet and hurried down the aisle between folding chairs filled with women, their feet hidden by shopping bags. They looked at her resentfully. Let them go shop, she thought, as she rolled up her sleeves.

Soon she was ready to go to restaurants. Two-star. Three-star. For this she needed certain men. A good meal was not enough, she soon discovered. The food was overrated. Environment was everything. The best dinners stood out in her mind like exquisitely lit paintings at an art gallery. There was the dinner at Café des Artistes with Edward, the financial analyst. He ordered the wine in French, using his hands, making expert bird sounds in his throat. He knew how to cut and eat a fresh fig. So this was what the food reviewer meant by "supernal." The way the fig sat on her tongue and melted around the edges, and the faintest gritty pop as the seeds crunched under her back teeth.

The kind of man who could afford to take her to such restaurants sometimes said disturbing things. "I'm tracking well at Shearson," Edward had said on their first date, leaving in the middle of the terrine to call his broker. This was not the kind of man you could talk to, but she could listen as she ate. She liked expense account dinners. The way you could order without worrying. The way you felt grateful to your date but not indebted. It was really some large corporation like Smith Barney or First Boston taking you out.

She never wanted to go back to the men's apartments. After a two hundred dollar meal, men sometimes expected it. Even if it was expense account. Things seemed drab after the restaurant. The glow of good eating was gone. She preferred making love first, then eating. Anticipating dinner afterwards made the end of sex less lonely.

She had met Edward on her lunch hour at the stand-up coffee bar at Bloomingdale's, sipping the daily coffee, Colombia Armenia Supremo with cinnamon.

"It's got a nice nose on it, and it finishes very well," he said. "But I stand by Melitta drip Vienna Roast, myself," he said.

"Actually, I drink instant." She stared right into his small, green eyes.

He laughed appreciatively. "My name's Edward. May I buy you another?"

Edward liked to involve food in their sex. He made his own massage oil by simmering, then steeping, fresh rosemary in extra virgin cold-pressed olive oil for twenty-four hours. He kept another homemade massage cream, a whipped yogurt base with pieces of naturally astringent fresh papaya, in his fridge that was full of condiments with foreign labels. He grew edible flowers in two window boxes on his terrace. Once he placed nasturtiums between each of her toes and ate them, one by one.

Edward liked calling her from his car phone. He also sent her faxes from his Park Avenue office about their dates. "In reference to our meeting at the above-captioned restaurant," one began. She hoped it was his secretary who had written this.

One Friday night he took her to a black-tie balsamic vinegar tasting at Palio. All around her men in tuxedos and women in black velvet sipped from paper soufflé cups, each holding a quarter-inch of vinegar imported from Modena, Italy. Edward, small and neat inside his tux, swished the vinegar around in his mouth, looking thoughtful. He wrote in tiny secretive handwriting in a miniature leather-bound notebook tucked next to his plate. "Note the balance, the complexity, the viscosity of the must," he said, a sheen of black vinegar on his small, pursed mouth.

Edward showed her how to pull the vinegar back so that it hit the soft palate. She found it unpleasant. Even the most expensive vintage, a hundred dollars for three and a third ounces, stabbed right into the glands behind her ears, making her mouth fill with spit. They ate six courses, each made by a different chef with a different vinegar. In the filet of beef with capers and pomegranate sauce, she tasted hints of the cheap old-fashioned cider vinegar that she had in her kitchen cupboard at home, but she said nothing.

She worried that she had killed off her taste buds. Too much coffee, the five years she'd smoked, harsh toasted bagels scraping the sensitivity out of her palate, scallion cream cheese and butter pecan cones dulling and clogging her senses. Food people had to be like racehorses: alert and keen. Although, she'd heard that a well-known restaurateur sometimes ate cold leftover Fettucine Alfredo from her own garbage pail in the middle of the night. It scared her the way food could turn on you like that.

Bill had given her the most delicate of orgasms. As his head disappeared under the covers, leaving her staring up at the ceiling in hopeless anticipation, her mind played tricks on her. When his big work boots returned to focus near her head, his oily jeans pulled low to show the waistband of his underwear, she blinked, surprised to see him. It always amazed her that such delicacy could come from him.

One evening at supper time, Bill brought their blackened charred camping saucepan from stove to table, placing it between their plates on a threadbare potholder.

"Get that dirty thing out of here," she'd screamed, walking into

the kitchen. The sight of his faded bandanna frothing from the
back pocket of his jeans, filthy and jaunty, enraged her. How fool-
ish of her to be hiding champagne and chocolate truffles in the
fridge for dessert.

"What's wrong?" He looked up at her, truly puzzled. This was
her problem. If she put out candles and place mats, he made fun of
her. Porcini, chanterelles, and morels were "fungus." When she
tried describing an article she'd read on risottos, about the careful
blending of stock and time and temperature, the watchful eye, the
achieving of just the right creamy texture, he grunted and said,
"Sounds like rice pudding."

On his birthday, as a surprise, she took him to a two-star
restaurant. The beautiful, golden-haired waiter in the floor-length
white apron, a three-foot pepper mill in his belt, stood at their
table reciting the specials.

"Tonight we have duck confit and shitake mushroom eggrolls
and gourgons of sea bass with rosemary pasta in zinfandel sauce."

"I'll have a cheeseburger," joked Bill.

The waiter's smile was sweet and pitying. Like an altar boy, he
grated the parmigiano high above the arugula salads. She knew he
was gay, but she wanted to be going home with him. He would
serve cognac in large goldfish goblets and warm it in his long-
fingered hands and kiss the insides of her wrists and the arches of
her feet—sensitive, out-of-the-way places like that.

When she didn't think about Bill, she hardly even remembered
that there was sex. Peak sexual experiences seemed like something
for the movies, for literature, for self-help books, for certain
women who needed to see themselves engaged with an orgasmic
life force. The most violent jolting orgasms she'd ever had were
with a vibrator she'd bought through an Eve's Garden catalogue.

It arrived in her mailbox wrapped in brown paper, but she had still blushed violently in her empty hallway. These orgasms were so quick, so intense, they were closer to electrocution. Her body arched and charged and she trembled so much afterwards she could hardly stand.

But it was an addiction. She could squeeze out an orgasm before heading out the door late to work. Once, when Edward was on his way up the stairs to take her to The Sign of the Dove for dinner, she stood in her bedroom in the dark, her dress pulled to her waist. There was a flush in her cheeks when she answered the door, and her hands trembled. "You're looking very well," Edward had said.

When she tried to touch herself, she was filled with impatience. It seemed slow and distant, as though her flesh had been numbed to the delicacy of minute sensation. She wondered if she shared the fate of men whose bellies leaned over jackhammers all day—she was scrambling her insides. One day, after a particularly explosive orgasm, she went to the kitchen drawer and took out a pair of poultry shears and cut the cord of the vibrator near the base. She regretted this impulsive castration the next day, but hadn't yet sent away for another one.

When the fugu shipment came to New York, she immediately called Edward. He'd hired a Japanese exchange student to teach them how to correctly use the sets of inlaid ivory chopsticks he carried in a velvet-lined case at the bottom of his briefcase. She caught him on his car phone, stuck in traffic outside the Lincoln Tunnel.

"Make pre-theater reservations at Petrossian and after-theater reservations at Nippon," he instructed. He was eating lunch. She imagined baguette crumbs showering into his lap. He'd have cov-

ered his Brooks Brothers slacks with one of the two teal-blue linen
napkins he kept in the glove compartment, along with a cork-
screw, two condoms and *The New Times Gourmet Shopper.*

She went home early from work and took a bath and dressed
all in black Lycra and put on layers of dusky gold eye shadow.
She'd read that a hundred people a year dropped dead in Japan
from eating improperly prepared blowfish, the flesh contaminated
by contact with the entrails or ovaries. The risk was part of the
dining experience.

That night at Petrossian, the caviar and champagne emporium
now favored by Edward for their after-work rendezvouses, they
sat next to an Arab man with two women. "Call girls," said
Edward, leaning over to whisper in her ear as he scooped smoked
sturgeon from the Caspian Sea onto a thin sliver of toast. A few
pearly gray fish roe were stuck in the corner of Edward's mouth.
He wasn't the kind of man who would appreciate it if she leaned
over and licked them off with her tongue.

When Edward went to the men's room, she looked up at the
handsome, dark-skinned young busboy with the beautiful mouth
as he refilled her water glass. She was sure she saw him look scorn-
fully at the silvery fish eggs lost on large white plates. She looked
at Edward as he crossed the dining room and sat down. Picking up
his napkin, he dabbed at his lips, smiling at her. Food made him
feel romantic.

When she saw large white linen napkins, she always thought of
Bill's huge, strong, black-nailed hands, imagined the napkin
tucked into his battered leather belt where he could smear his
hands on it as though it was a mechanic's rag. Bill used strange
things as napkins. Dish towels. T-shirts. He blew his nose in napkins at restaurants. Once, when she complained, he dipped a
twisted corner of the napkin into his water glass, leaned over and

gently wiped her mouth, smiling at her. Bill wouldn't know how to delicately bite the head off a quail and suck politely at the skull, like Edward.

She hadn't really enjoyed the fugu, although she'd quite enjoyed the faint numb feeling the fish had left around her lips and tongue. She rubbed a piece of pickled ginger over her lips, relishing the silky, slimy feel, and took a sip of sake. She felt full, but still hungry, the way she often did when they'd eaten two (once even three) meals at different restaurants spaced throughout the evening. After such evenings she sometimes felt guilty.

The overhead spotlight at Nippon shone down on the smooth, almost hairless top of Edward's head. In contrast, the hairs on his fingers as they held lacquered black chopsticks, tweezing at the air, gleamed as though dusted with gold powder. He very deliberately placed his last piece of sushi in the center of his mouth with his chopsticks, having carefully created an edifice of wasabi and pickled ginger around it.

Edward didn't really like sushi. Once, coming back from the ladies' room, approaching their table from behind, she saw him furtively unroll his yellowtail and scallion hand roll and examine the piece of fish as though he was looking inside a diaper. In the same way, she felt the faintest unease from him as he delicately removed her underwear. He did this the way a woman might, inching her panties down over each hip, first one side, then the other. She imagined, as he rooted around in her pubic hair, that he was picking out leaves and twigs and fuzzy bits from a bowl of berries and placing them on the edge of the bowl. She was sure she did not entirely please the refined mysteries of Edward's palate. She was used to Bill's robust, sweeping tug as he stood at her feet, the underwear rolling into a neat, tight figure eight, and tossed into a corner of the room. Edward liked women who were more like birds, or boys. She'd watched his eyes follow thin, flat-chested blondes in pearls and low navy heels as they crossed restaurants and went into the ladies' room. She sometimes felt when he labored over her own breasts that he wished they weren't there.

Edward kissed her in the cab on the way back to his apartment. His tongue was cold and his breath faintly fishy. The fugu had excited him. Upstairs, he asked her to undress, handing her one of the matching kimonos he'd bought at a boutique on the Upper West Side, and disappeared into the kitchen. For months he'd told her he'd been wanting to try something he'd seen in a Japanese noodle western known for its erotic food scenes. It had to be after they'd had sushi. Edward enjoyed theme evenings.

He walked slowly into the bedroom balancing a tray holding a blue and white sake carafe, two matching porcelain cups, a martini glass and a white washcloth. At the bottom of the glass was a large white egg. Placing the tray on the bed, he jumped onto the middle and sat cross-legged facing her. Carefully wiping the outside of the egg with the washcloth, he cracked it sharply against the rim of the martini glass and then began transferring the yolk back and forth between the two half-shells. The egg white streamed thickly down into a blue Japanese soup bowl. Separating the last strands of albumen with his fingers, he plopped the bare yolk into the martini glass and delicately wiped his fingers on the washcloth. Through the side of the glass she could see a faint membrane on the yolk and the tiniest speck of blood.

Edward poured sake into their cups, took a sip from his, removed his glasses, then picked up the glass. *"Kanpai,"* he said, slowly tipping the egg yolk into his mouth. He made a slight, gagging movement with his chest, then became very still. He moved slowly toward her, his green eyes crossed down, as though following the path of the yolk. He gestured for her to come closer. When their lips were almost touching, he turned his head sideways. She could feel his tongue urging the yolk out of his mouth and into hers. It broke on their lips and dribbled down their chins onto Edward's maroon and fawn Ralph Lauren comforter. She looked down and saw his kimono open to reveal the two white rinds of his heels where his feet crossed, and his small, limp penis. She worried about salmonella for the next twenty-four hours.

She hadn't always been afraid of eating alone. When she was in a good mood, she made up a tray complete with place mat and cloth napkin and sat in front of the TV on her bed trying to take small bites. Sometimes, if the meal felt elegant, she would enjoy a sense of well-being, of independence, usually when there was wine. But she was afraid of choking. You couldn't help hearing all those stories. Mama Cass Elliot on her turkey sandwich. All those people you actually knew who had to be given the Heimlich maneuver. Once she practiced giving it to herself by pressing against the wall, her fist jammed into her rib cage. What famous writer had choked and died on a bottle cap? All kinds of things could end up in your mouth.

So much was unnatural now. People thought grains and beans were romantic. And the baby vegetables. Miniature squashes and broccolis and Brussels sprouts that looked like they belonged in an elf's garden. $8.99, $11.99 a pound. Impossible prices, yet so little and perfect. Not like the grotesque clones they were creating now, chickens with bulbous breasts for extra white meat. And the hormones. Edward had ordered carpaccio of beef one night and she'd hardly been able to eat it. What made the meat so bright red and even-grained? She'd had to spit out a chewed-up piece, all mixed up with capers, into her napkin when Edward wasn't looking, because she felt her throat closing. So many things in this city were unnatural. Like eating outside. People walking right by, models and dancers carrying big battered leather bags, and leaning down into your plate, staring right at your food. All those eating disorders walking by and wanting what was on your plate.

Strange things like this made her miss Bill. The way, when they were sitting on the sofa, he balanced his plate on her head and carefully scraped the fork over the plate so that she could feel the tines on her skull through the tin plate gently vibrating. He was the only man whose lap she could fall asleep in.

One night, Edward answered the door wearing a white chef's apron. There were faint smears of what looked like blood down the front. Just that morning she'd gotten her period, and all day she'd been feeling angry at Edward, anticipating his distaste. Bill had enjoyed her menstrual blood, had watched it pool and flower in the toilet bowl or on a sheet with the interest of a zoologist studying animal droppings. He had once held her blood on his finger to her lips, making her taste it.

She knew Edward was making pâté for their first course. She wanted him to take her out to dinner. Pâté frightened her, with its mysterious brownish layers of organs, finely ground to velvet, dotted with pieces of dark feral mushroom, and the musty slime it left on her tongue.

Edward's butcher block table was strewn with small bodies. "I'm using squab, duck and quail livers for my forcemeat," Edward said, picking up a pair of thin surgical gloves from a box on the kitchen counter and pulling them over his hands. He smoothed them at the wrists. Underneath she could see the blond hairs, matted down and swirled into patterns. He picked up the livers and began separating them with the very tips of his fingers. The gloves were instantly stained dark red. The pieces of liver looked tiny and vulnerable. She felt herself twinge down there, imagining her own blood clots, dark terrifying clumps of herself, detaching.

"This is a squab," said Edward, picking up the small blue headless body and holding it out to her on the palm of his hand. She didn't know what he wanted from her. Reaching out, she stroked the pimply violet skin. With one gloved finger, he pushed the skin back to show her the brownish meat underneath. He still held the bird out. She took it from him as she would a baby, both hands under the frail armpits. The squab hung down between them, small thighs folding in on each other. Instinctively, she sat it on the edge of the butcher block counter where it was transformed into a tiny deformed child. She jiggled the tips of its wings, so that the elbows seesawed. She giggled.

"Careful! You'll tear the breast," said Edward sharply.

He took the squab from her and laid it down next to the quail and the duck so that the three bodies were lined up side by side as though on gurneys.

He pulled another pair of surgical gloves from the box and held them out to her. "Would you like to help prepare the garlic custard?"

"Yes," she said, nodding.

She didn't want to cook. She didn't want to find herself apologizing for the blood later.

She watched Edward select a small knife and test it against the edge of his thumb. Pulling on a new pair of gloves, he cut a neat slit in the head of a perfectly formed clove of garlic.

Tonight she was hungry, and she didn't want to eat alone. Edward was away on a business trip. Bill was somewhere in the city, too far away to touch. She took a taxi to the Oyster Bar. Here she felt safe, the way the long cement ramps led down to the restaurant, giving it an air-raid shelter feel. She only had eight dollars. After studying the blackboard menu for a long time, she ordered two Belon and one Wellfleet oyster. She liked bluepoints, but she'd heard somewhere that oysters from New York coastal waters were the most contaminated.

It was hard to eat oysters slowly. If she chewed them too much, she started thinking about what she was eating. The oysters turned into a slimy mush in her mouth and her gag reflex was activated. She picked up the first Belon and brought the shell to her lips, enjoying the sharp, rough seashore feel, so foreign and special in the middle of the city. She closed her eyes and took the last tiny briny sip that had collected in the bottom of the shell. Placing it carefully back on her plate so it wouldn't clatter, she braced the shell between her thumb and forefinger, and scraped with her cocktail fork at the slight rubbery piece of flesh that was still left. If she thought about oysters too much, she started envisioning the polluted crannies where they nestled, absorbing poisons. She alternated between shells with her fork, eating handfuls of oyster crackers with cocktail sauce and horseradish in between, and sipping her water. She wished she could afford a glass of wine.

The Oyster Bar was full for a Thursday evening, and she worried about taking up a seat for too long. But she didn't want to leave. A wide, beef-red face in square gold glasses had started on his second dozen next to her. She tried not to eye them. When you ordered a dozen oysters, they served them in a huge iron shell, the oysters nestled into a mound of shaved ice like separate gifts.

A man buying you oysters wasn't quite the same as a man buying you drinks at the bar, even though he bought her wine, too. First, he asked her executive-from-out-of-town questions. Then he ordered her two of every oyster on the blackboard menu. She stopped worrying about saying no, and thank you, and you shouldn't. She stopped worrying about eating them slowly and scraping the connective tissues from the shells and clacking them together like a poor starving castanet player to make sure they were dry of juice. She gulped and slid them down, not even stopping to savor the differences. The deep-fried softshell crabs arrived with two lemon halves tied in red net bags with yellow string, their legs tangled and crispy with batter. Impossible to avoid the intimacy of sharing a tureen of lobster bisque thick with cream and oil beads red as iodine floating on the surface. She tried, by leaning away from him after each spoonful.

"I don't normally do this kind of thing," he said in the elevator on the way up to his room at the Grand Hyatt next door.

"I don't either," she said, giggling. She rubbed at the raised gold fuzz on the wallpaper inside the elevator, noticing that her fingers felt distant, fuzzy, from the three glasses of wine.

A crisp, anonymous raincoat was draped over an armchair near the entrance to the suite. Fruit in an ornate silver bowl sat on a long, low sideboard next to a wide-screen television. The lighting was soft and yellow. She thought of Bill, wondering, with the sudden piercing sentimentality she sometimes felt when she'd been drinking wine, what he was doing at just that exact moment. She saw him hunched over in front of the TV, his feet in thin, grayish socks up on the old wooden kitchen chair, eating a bowl of cereal mounded with fruit.

The man ordered champagne, loosening his tie as he stood at the table beside the bed, a gesture so familiar she knew it was from the movies. The champagne arrived on a trolley in a tall cylindrical cooler the murky yellow of dental plastic. There was no ice, just an empty tube of air and space that left the base of the Clicquot dry. He poured the champagne into tall fluted glasses, the stems balanced expertly between different fingers of one hand.

She gulped three glasses. He drank quickly, too, his mouth opened wide so she could see through the bottom of the glass, his teeth wolfish and slightly yellow. Strange, to see a stranger's fillings. They ate fruit from the fruit bowl, standing over it. He unbuttoned her blouse. He tucked bunches of grapes into her bra. He took a banana and unzipped his pants, holding the fruit in front of himself. They started laughing. She felt herself wetting her pants and squeezed the tops of her legs together. She went to lie on the bed, feeling dizzy. He moved toward her, peeling the banana, humming bump and grind music, his damp red upper lip puffing out in horn sounds. When the banana first entered her, she could feel the cool soft tip from a great distance. But the banana was too ripe. She felt it give and lose its shape as he pushed slowly. He kept pushing until his palm was flat against her, massaging round and round in circles. The smell of banana rose between them, sweet and rotten.

He sat down next to her on the bed. He carefully twisted two grapes from the bunches tucked in her bra and placed one, then the other, over each nipple so that they stood up straight inside her bra. Looking into her eyes, using both hands, he squeezed the grapes with a single hard pinching motion. She felt the cold trickle of the juice roll down the side of each breast into the underwire of her bra.

"My fruit princess," he said, leaning close enough for her to feel his sharp, winey breath on her face.

She accepted the fifty-dollar bill for the cab ride downtown and gave the driver a big tip. Standing in front of her apartment building, she stuffed the rest of the bills into a crisp roll in her change purse. She couldn't go home.

She walked ten blocks farther downtown to Two Brothers' coffee shop. Sliding into one of the back booths, she stared across at the dirty orange bench where she used to rest her feet in Bill's lap. Between bites he would massage her feet with his big hands, digging his fingers between her toes so that by the end of the meal her socks looked like finger puppets.

She ordered a turkey sandwich and french fries. The food arrived too quickly. The plate of french fries was huge. They poked up at her, glistening with fat. She looked up and saw the waiter sitting at a small table smoking a cigarette, watching her. She picked up the sandwich, feeling her meal from the Oyster Bar rise in a rich tide to the base of her throat, then recede.

SWEAT

THE GYM GETS SURREAL THIS LATE AT NIGHT. THE CEILINGS become low as a dungeon's, the equipment grows heavier and stronger, the straps hang down from the padded seats, ready for executions. The music is either very loud, as though no one is in charge, or turned off completely so that the clanging of weights and the occasional agonized groan echoes mournfully. The mood is alternately festive and a little frightening; the mother has given up and gone to bed without turning off the lights.

There is loneliness here at night. The frantic energy disappears with the six to eight o'clock crowd. Those who are left cling to their machines, tucked low as jockeys. They are wet with sweat and exhausted, their fingers stained with print from other people's wrinkled, tidemarked newspapers abandoned on seats and handlebars. She has sometimes fallen asleep on a machine, slipping into a doze, slanted backward on the Roman chair, eyes closed, hands crossed over her chest. The way her leotard is stained dark, she might have been shot.

When she first joined the gym, she automatically became part of the brisk early evening set, arriving after work and before supper, an aerobics class or fifteen desultory minutes on the stationary bike barely arousing a flush on her body. The gym was crowded and bustling then; members glanced frequently at the wall clock or at large waterproof skindiver's watches and frowned slightly, accelerating their speed. She imagined that someone was waiting for them at a restaurant, or that they had baked potatoes at home in the oven or children waiting to be tucked in. She found herself looking up at the clock and hunching with renewed purpose over the handlebars of the Lifecycle as though she, too, had pressing plans. Even in the beginning, she never felt like one of them, someone who had sensibly allotted an exact amount of time for exercise, calculating precisely how many minutes she needed to work out to achieve aerobic maintenance: to burn the fat, but not deplete the blood sugar. She had never been able to adopt the vocabulary of the gym, couldn't bring herself to talk about *working in* and *spotting* and *dumbbell curls* and *incline flyes*. These were people who had plans for the future of their bodies, the way they invested in real estate or sound stocks. She had no plan. She hadn't yet learned that she loved to sweat.

Tonight she has started out on the Lifecycle. Opposite her, the Dripper is riding the StairMaster. It is somehow her fate to get on the StairMaster after the Dripper. When he's finished, there are always two lakes underneath the foot pedals on the black rubber matting with its truck-tire pattern. He doesn't seem to notice. He ejects a long streamer of brown paper towel from the dispenser and carefully wipes down the machine everywhere but underneath, as though it's his horse. It used to make her feel queasy, watching her own drops of sweat join the lake of his. She used to worry that someone might think that it was she who had sweat that much.

She has thought of going up to the Dripper and politely asking him to wipe up the puddles underneath the StairMaster, but this seems squeamish. Especially now that she wears leather weight-lifting gloves in a commanding chestnut brown and a wide leather belt to protect her lower back, so new and stiff it feels like a saddle around her waist. Complaining about the amount of a man's sweat seems excessively feminine given the kinds of strides she now plans to make at the gym; in fact, has already made. She wipes up after him and says nothing. She knows she is jealous. She has come to think of the machine he is riding, bending low, breathing hard, as hers. Secretly, she watches, as though witnessing infidelity.

It has happened over the last six months that she has been coming to the gym later and later at night. It has started to interfere with her job. She wakes up in the morning stiff and exhausted, muscles cramped. She lurches and stumbles like an old woman when she climbs out of bed, then straightens out slowly, still half asleep, lifting her T-shirt to pose before the mirror, flexing the muscles that she has worked the night before, sucking in her resting abdomen so that she can see her progress. Often now, she arrives at work half an hour late or more and sits at her desk rolling her neck and kneading her calves, trying to loosen herself. Performing calisthenics under her desk, she squeezes the palms of her hands together, keeping the cords of her neck relaxed, undetectable.

Throughout the day, she opens her canvas bag and leans down to breathe in the gym: the musty vacuumed stink of gray carpeting, cementy locker-room smells of feet, eucalyptus, chlorine, Windex, metal, sweat, the dried secretions of her own body. She used to do this at work with underwear stuffed into her bag after a night with a lover; lean down and inhale the smell of black lace panties streaked white with sex, bringing back the evening before.

Now she touches the damp ball of clothes as though feeling a lover. She no longer seems to miss the other.

At first it seemed strange, unnatural, to come to the gym after nine o'clock at night. She arrived bundled in sweatpants, a sweat-shirt and thick socks, carrying a bath towel. She couldn't wait to get home. Now she stays later than even the mid-evening exercis-ers, the ones who leave by ten. They are more leisurely than the earlier group, flirtatious and talkative, prepared to stand in small groups and chat between sets as though they are at a cocktail party. She watches them from across the gym, surprised that they spend so much time discussing body parts. She hears them comparing notes, arguing about whether exercising at night keeps them awake. There is a school of thought that maintains that this is a stimulus to the system, much like drinking several espressos right before bed. After a strenuous workout, they lie awake all night lis-tening to their systems buzzing. Others will say that they find it like drinking a glass of warm milk. They can go right home and float into bed on a tide of endorphins.

When she first started going to the gym, she would gorge on heavy food right after working out. One night, standing up, still wearing her weight-lifting gloves, she devoured leftover lamb vin-daloo and drank over half a bottle of cabernet sauvignon, enjoying the way the wine and food prickled her already flushed cheeks, filled her stretched, aching body. At the gym the next day, she could feel the spices and alcohol rumbling around looking for an outlet. By the time she reached the middle of her thirty-minute cycle on the StairMaster, the smell of curry had soaked into the leotard under her arms and her favorite sweat patch between her breasts. Now she prefers it when she has been drinking only seltzer and eating clean raw salads so that her sweat smells like bleach. Although she is ravenous when she gets home, often after midnight, especially if she's sat in both the steam room and the sauna, she stands in front of the open refrigerator and stares at the bottles of seltzer and mineral water lining the shelves in clear blue rows, imagining herself suspended inside.

Peter, the young man from India who is the night manager, has sometimes let her stay at the gym beyond eleven o'clock closing. He allows her to dawdle among the machines or stretch out on a mat, and then linger in the deserted women's dressing room, opening and closing empty lockers, looking for things people might have left behind. Peter likes the company, she thinks. He is premed at Columbia. He always has Gray's *Anatomy* open at the front desk, studying charts of human bones, muscles and ligaments, holding on to both sides of a small white towel draped around the back of his smooth brown neck. From the StairMaster, she watches him, his hair a shining blue-black wing under the fluorescent lights. Every half hour, he comes out onto the floor and straps on his weight-lifting belt and does a few bench presses and biceps curls, a modern study avoidance technique, the equivalent of getting up and going to the fridge for a snack. She knows he doesn't begin his serious working out until twelve-thirty or one in the morning, long after the gym has closed.

At eleven o'clock, he locks the doors and he no longer has to keep track of membership cards and locks and towels. She envisions him standing in the middle of the empty floor under a solitary lighted section of the gym. Perhaps he takes his shirt off. She likes to imagine that he works out in total silence, except for the hiss of his exhalations. She hears him reciting the names of muscles between clenched teeth as he does his reps, *trapezius, latissimus dorsi, pectoralis major,* imprinting them in his memory. Probably he plays loud rock music.

Peter's white sweat suit makes his skin look like creamy mocha

icing. She finds his mouth girlish and beautiful, pursed in a permanent kiss shape, yet he keeps his eyes deliberately hooded and
injects a tough gleam into them, seeking out women's eyes with
careless arrogance, sometimes not looking at them at all. A gym
is a strange place for someone who looks like a young raja.
Sometimes she catches him turning and looking at his muscles in
the long mirrors, but in a different way than the others, as though
he is not only studying the definition, but noting to which muscle
group they belong. Sometimes she catches him looking at her. It is
Peter who introduced her to the StairMaster, who has taught her
the composition of sweat.

The Dripper is still bent low over the StairMaster, his weight
distributed along the shoulders, his face leaning down and turned
sideways in concentration. She can see the drops hanging from his
fingertips where they drape loosely over the console. If she were
sensible, she wouldn't wait for him to finish. She would use the
Gauntlet instead. Hercules is right now on one of these machines,
his huge thighs trembling with each step. The Gauntlet is never
quite the same, its endless cycle of actual moving stairs depresses
her. They feel too authentic, too much like the long climb up the
subway stairs to work when the escalator has broken down, and
she arrives at the top gasping for air, her body drained, the lactic
acid pooling and burning her joints. It is as though all the training
she's done, all those thousands of flights she has climbed at the
gym amount to nothing at all in the mundane world of real stairs.
In the same way, the newly bursting muscles in her arms seem arti-
ficial, something that won't prove to be useful or assist with sur-
vivalist feats of strength, like opening jars or pulling someone
from the subway tracks.

When she first started working out, her body happily performed its minimal exertions under cover. It was mostly the heat

that drove her to undress one night, the rise in her body temperature and the feeling of hanging wet cotton, that made her step off the StairMaster in panic, stripping off her outer layer of clothes and climbing back onto the machine before the two-minute grace period was up and the program terminated. Wearing only a leotard and tights, she felt suddenly light and free under the ceiling fan, the tiny hairs on the back of her neck stirring, the heap of wet gray cotton abandoned on the floor next to her. Now she wears only unitards of black or industrial gray cotton with a small enough percentage of Lycra not to interfere with her body's breathing. This shows up the sweat marks immediately. She presses the material against her body to bring up the dampness. What is the point unless you can see what you have accomplished? The feel of these clothes is unlike anything she knows, like wearing nothing at all, but more comfortable because she is safe and protected. She no longer washes her workout clothes every night, but will step into them again the next evening, sometimes slightly damp from the night before, and the musty coolness massages her skin, a living membrane.

Sometimes her sweat leaves jagged hieroglyphics against the black material, under the arms, across her chest and back and around her crotch. She stares at the marks, tracing them with a finger, then sponges them away and wears the unitard again, as though adding to the accumulation of a history. She has started to study the patterns of sweat on other people's bodies, certain she will learn something revealing about their lives.

Peter tips back in his chair, his balance assisted by the way he braces the small white towel around his neck, and looks up at her. She has asked him for an UltraFuel from the glass-doored refrigerator behind the desk, but he has brought her a Carbo Force instead. She is not sure of the difference, although she knows that they are both ergogenic recovery drinks that replace potassium. Peter says it's like drinking the equivalent of sweat, but more expensive. He flips open the lid as though he's opening a beer. These drinks are as dense and lethal as sugared iced tea, but the lift is perceptible. Usually she drinks one before getting on the StairMaster. She refuses to carry around her own small Evian or Volvic. The ridged plastic bottles look medical to her, something that should be turned upside down and connected to an IV.

"Are you having a good workout today?" Peter has the polite manners of the proprietor of a posh British hotel. His eyes are flat and black and extremely diffident, as though to mask the roil of contempt twisting behind them. She suspects that there are generations of British boarding schools in his genes.

Mother-to-Be is standing at the desk gulping a Recharge. She hasn't missed a workout since she started to show. Her walk is unchanged, the awkward, duck-toed glide of a teenage ballerina; her weight belt is strapped low under her belly. She has the perfectly carved arms of a marble statue. "The baby loves these electrolyte replacers," she says, the powdery column of her neck working. She never seems to sweat, even when she's bench pressing close to her own weight.

Peter has turned up the music and started to clean the mirrors. It's fifteen minutes until closing time. Closing time used to mean dash-out-of-the-office and drinks. She detaches the long iron bar on the cross-chest pulley and lays it on the floor alongside the mirror. Adjusting the weight to ten pounds on each side, she hooks the two handles to either pulley. Standing in the middle of the floor-to-ceiling frame, facing the mirror, both arms stretched out so that her sockets feel a satisfying pressure, she takes a deep breath. Her underarms look pulled out, slightly distended. She lifts the weights off the stand, just enough so that she can see the tension in her chest and deltoids, the movement under her skin reptilian and mysterious. The demarcation, like armor plate between her breasts, has not yet fully formed. Bending slightly at the waist, keeping her head raised so that she can watch, she brings both pulleys in together, trying to keep the pressure even. She crosses her wrists in front of her thighs and holds them there for a moment so that both the cables and her arms tremble. The belt cuts into her waist and under her breasts, safe and painful. Sometimes she forgets to breathe.

After three sets of fifteen reps, her chest feels filled with air, swollen, pleasantly irritated. Her arms shake imperceptibly at her sides and her waist feels damp as she walks to the cooler for a drink of water. She looks over at the StairMaster and then up at the clock. The Dripper is still stepping rapidly, his mouth open and gasping up toward the ceiling fan. She hates the ferocious way he steps. He has never stayed so late. She presses her *pectoralis major,* digging in her fingers, anticipating the soreness tomorrow, and returns to the empty frame where the pulleys dangle.

Placing a forty-five-pound plate on either side of the leg extension machine, she lowers herself into the seat, which has the slant and awkwardness of a cockpit. She removes the two pins that stop the platform at a certain level, wanting it to come down as low as possible, to push her haunches into her belly, to feel the eerie splitting pressure at the base of her spine, the chemical gathering of strength in her thighs, as she raises the platform above her head. From between her parted knees, as she slowly brings the platform down, she sees Hercules, framed between the cold blue bars. A huge flat weight is now hooked onto his head by a woven headpiece like a gladiator's helmet and hangs down in front of him. He nods slowly, doing neck lifts, his eyes watering, his face and corded neck the colors of raw beef. Their lifting and pushing becomes synchronized. His eyes meet hers unblinkingly each time he lifts his head.

The Dripper has finished. Balanced on the pedals of the StairMaster, locked in the upright position, he wiped down the console and the silver handlebars with a black hand towel. Finally, he stepped back and off the machine and over the two puddles underneath. The gym is now empty. She hadn't noticed the last person leave, hadn't noticed when Peter turned off the main lights. He sits with his head bent under a solitary light that casts a bluish glow over the entire gym. The free weights are now neatly arranged, lined up in rows by size, from the five-pound dumbbells to the huge hundred-pounders. Without streaks, the mirrors gleam as though under water. Perfectly still, the Nautilus and Universal machines look huge and waiting. As she walks up to the front desk, she touches the hanging bars, starting up an iron whispering. Without looking up, Peter pushes a Carbo Force and two fresh towels over the counter. He closes his Gray's *Anatomy* and pulls the white towel from around his neck. He glances at his watch, then stands up and stretches.

"Ready?" he says.

She downs half the Carbo Force in three long gulps. She hadn't realized how thirsty she was. "Ready," she says, not sure what she is answering.

Peter seems bigger than he does during the day, stronger. He's looking straight into her eyes. She wonders for a moment if he will hurt her, and then dismisses the thought. This is Peter, who studies bones and ligaments and tendons; who spends half the night folding small white towels hot from the drier neatly into thirds like Japanese washcloths.

He steps down from the raised platform on which the desk sits and walks behind her and stops. She can feel his breath on the back of her neck. She doesn't know if she wants him to touch her.

"Did you know that a child is born with three hundred and fifty bones and that some of them fuse together so that an adult has only two hundred and six?" he asks.

She shakes her head, then closes her eyes, tips back her head, and empties the bottle. The ends of her hair brush his chest. Her biceps mount the bone of her upper arms and recede. Lately, her muscles have a separate life of their own. She turns toward him. She's seen how he spots for the men at the gym as they lift their huge weights; how he crouches behind them like a midwife, tenderly bracing their trembling arms. She can feel how his slender brown hands will weigh down her midriff as she strains up on the slant board. He will kneel before her as she straddles the bench doing preacher curls, the meat of her arms and legs spread against the black leather. She can hear him counting the sets and reps. He will blot the sweat from her forehead and neck. He will count in her ear, whisper that she isn't pushing hard enough.

Gathering the two towels, she reenters the gym, Peter following. Stopping in front of the StairMaster, she slings a towel around its shoulders, then drops to one knee to retie her cross-trainers. In front of her, the two shallow lakes beneath the StairMaster gleam in the half-light, strangely bottomless. Reaching out, her hand hovers just above the larger puddle, then skims lightly down, grazing its surface. She binds this hand in a towel for a moment, making a huge stump, and squeezes hard, then throws the towel onto the floor. Knowing by feel what to do, she mounts the StairMaster, the lights guiding her as if it were a runway. She rests her hands on the edge of the console, and stares into the restless pattern of red lights.

Under the one overhead spotlight nearby, Peter kneels, fitting cuffs onto the largest barbell. He looks up at her in the mirror, seeming to stare at her through the darkness. She has grown used to watching people at the gym through the reflection of her own body. Looking away, she tries to fix a point of concentration.

Her legs pump, and she begins to breathe faster. Her mouth opens slightly, her lips and tongue already pleasantly dry. It always begins up there, at the same place at the top of her scalp, a distant, slipping sensation that floods her with relief. It is this feeling, the beginning of something that will end exactly where she knows it will, that she has begun to live for. After five minutes, a single drop of sweat separates from the crown of her head and begins to travel down. She concentrates on its path down the left side of her neck toward her breasts. This first drop she never touches, but lets it slalom down her body. She used to pat the drops of sweat dry the moment they formed, ticklish as insect bites, towel bunched ready in her hand. Now she lets the sweat wander and stream from her body like rain. Part of the pleasure, she knows, is this familiarity.

At the moment the first drop disappears between her breasts, she raises her hand and presses her unitard there, trapping it. A bright spot forms. Her hair is beginning to hang and shrink, and she pushes it behind both ears, plastering it to her head. From across the gym, Peter is still staring at her. Often, he watches her with a blank look on his face. She tries to imagine him in different clothes, or no clothes at all.

She turns her head away quickly. The sweat has started to soak in at the tops of her legs, the last place that is still dry. This is the dangerous part, when her body demands to stop. For a moment she wraps both arms around the StairMaster and rests her forehead against it as though it is a wide rocky chest that can hold her up. Her breath is loud and tattered, her face so raw it could be bleeding. Looking down, she watches as one drop of sweat, then another, joins the Dripper's. She wraps her towel around her neck, twisting the two ends into a safe, rough tourniquet, then releases it.

Leaning in close, she inputs the codes again, this time to the maximum level. She has programmed the StairMaster for an hour. She feels calm, outside herself. She has left her second wind behind and moved into her third, as though entering a new body, the thing they talk about, the flow, the dream.

Peter is now lying on the bench, his knees raised, doing slow, deep bench presses, staring up at the ceiling. She shifts her gaze back to the darkened mirror. If she is to last, she must focus, pace herself. Peter has taught her about stamina. *Finished already?* His mocking voice lives inside her head.

A drop of sweat falls from her chin onto the StairMaster's black console and drips down. Without interrupting the steady churn of her legs, she leans down and darts out her tongue to catch it, the dried salt burning her lips.

Peter stands abruptly and pulls off his sweatshirt. Under the bright spotlight, his chest is totally smooth and brown, his nipples tiny and almost black, delicate as a girl's. He walks toward her, his white sweatpants drooping low on his body, resting just under his hip bones. Washboard. She knows they call it that. For a moment she sees the antique washboard her mother kept propped in the basement, with its rough metal ridges and sturdy wooden legs. She thinks of her favorite sheets, of bleeding steak with a glass of red wine, of a long black dress, of a man's hand cupping her once soft belly.

Peter veers suddenly over to the front desk and comes back toward her carrying a tower of white towels up to his chin. He has turned up the music very loud. He starts throwing the towels down onto the floor on either side of her StairMaster, wiping up the puddles with a circular motion of his foot, darting in and pulling away each time she steps down. Leaving the towels heaped beneath her, a dirty, ruined mountain range, he climbs onto the StairMaster next to hers. Eyes stinging, she watches sidelong as his fingers flutter in a delicate arpeggio over the program keys. Now both of their consoles are filled with lights. As he begins the first slow, robotic steps, she slows hers to match, trying to check her raspy breathing. It is important that they end together.

It is this she finds startling, the way her body flushes and prickles with heat. The wetness oozes out in private shapes and colors, staining, marking, a surprise to her each time. Her mouth opens involuntarily, and she makes little secret sounds. Peter echoes the sounds hoarsely. Their voices strain together, lost somewhere between pleasure and pain.

Fifty minutes.

From a tremendous height, she looks down at the terrain of heaped towels below her. She holds her two hands up in front of her, backlit so that the webs between her fingers shimmer with dampness, almost translucent.

Peter whips his head toward her, showering her in an arc of sweat.

"A thousand flights," he shouts over the music. "Let's do a thousand."

Her mind is empty, landing on thoughts for a moment, then slipping away into a cottony gray landscape.

If faintness or dizziness occur while operating this machine, stop immediately and seek help.

Her feet keep stepping.

At this moment, there is nothing in the world that she wants.

S N O O P

I FIND THE VIDEOS WRAPPED IN DOUBLE PLASTIC GROCERY bags inside a Timberland boot box in the back of his closet. I've become a snoop lately. I don't trust, have never trusted.

He's safely at work. I climb up on a chair and rummage in the closet among his sweaters and bicycle tubes and neatly folded squares of Christmas wrapping paper.

I slide *Pumped Love* into the VCR. Why did Charlie stop the tape here? I want to know at exactly what point he came, if he did come, lying back naked on the futon couch in the dark, not even a towel across himself for the benefit of the neighbors. I imagine him jerking off, which he refuses to do for me so I can watch. I wonder how long it takes, how he holds his hand. He hardly admits to doing this, although he loves to tease me with all the different names for it, all the hideous tortured descriptions that men come up with. He tells me with this courtly, polite look on his face that he thinks of me when he masturbates. Although this secretly pleases me, I tell him he's full of shit.

Rewinding the tape, just enough to give me some background, I press Play. There's a close-up of a woman's plum-black ass, round and bruised-looking. The sound of clanging weights, some-one's heavy breathing, fills Charlie's living room. I lower the volume and move closer. The camera pulls back. She's wearing black leather workout gloves and a choke collar. Cross-chest pul-leys and a long iron crossbar dangle behind her. Flanked on either side by a man, one white, one black, she lies back with one foot on either side of the gym bench and spreads her legs. She touches her breasts. They remain upright, two dark plastic bowls, her nipples stretched so tautly over silicone they seem to disappear. She pulls at them anyway, yanking them into points. She begins to moan.

The men stare down at her, expressionless. The one who stands facing her also straddles the bench, pushes inside her, his legs bent so he can reach that far down; the other, near her head, thrusts into her mouth. She turns her head sideways, straining her neck to reach him. Now both men stand over her. Her open mouth turns from one to the other, back and forth between lollipops. She makes the flat choked sound of a tongue trapped under a depressor. I press the Mute button on the remote and watch as they all come. The men's faces don't move. Their penises droop. The woman writhes unconvincingly, her mouth an O shape.

I leave the tape here, stopped at the exact place I found it. I press eject. Wrapping the video back in the two plastic FoodTown bags along with the others, I return it to the Timberland box and close the lid, carefully adjust the position of the box on the shelf, climb down, pull the chair back into the living room, get on my hands and knees to make sure there aren't scrape marks on the wood floor.

He has a way of staring at me that I can't read, his eyes a dark golden brown, and empty. I stare into them, waiting for a message from inside. If I move, if I budge, if I show fear, he'll dart away. I can't believe that there's nothing behind his gaze, that thoughts like mine aren't teeming and darting wildly around, thoughts of me. My best friend, Samantha, told me how she was driving along a highway, filled with misty, careful love for her husband and turned to him, touching her hand to his cheek.

"What are you thinking?" she asked.

"About Spitfire engines," he said.

Perhaps this is the difference between men and women?

I worry that I worship his body and that he hardly notices mine, except when he drags my breast to the top of my chest and takes my nipple in his mouth and brings the whole thing to youthful erectness as if blowing up a bicycle tire. Sometimes in the car as he drives, I stare mesmerized at the veins snaking beneath the skin on the inside of his forearms, fix on the patches of muscle, faintly pitted and beautiful under the smooth skin. Later, upstairs, I poke and prod him like a pork chop. I pound at him, pummel him, banging his chest with my fists, hit his solar plexus, the dead body sound making him only slightly flinch. I love feeling that he's mine. I flip his penis, tossing it from side to side, swat at it gently, then push down on it hard. I once read in a women's magazine that men complain that women treat their penises too gently. He's not really so sensitive unless I sit in just the wrong place in his lap and wriggle to position myself. One time I was sitting in an armchair after he'd come and he stood next to me and whipped me with it across the cheek like a rubber truncheon, making such a thick wet sound, stunning me, leaving a red weal across my face, then fell to his knees apologizing; he had no idea it would hurt, he thought it was no longer so hard, he was only playing. Perhaps this is, after all, what love is?

Comfort, they say, is the trade-off. Where is my comfort? Where is my sex when I need it? It's a Saturday afternoon and I'm lying on the floor of my apartment with my vibrator plugged into the living room socket where I usually plug in my vacuum cleaner. A mountain of clothes sits by the door. I should be doing laundry. I stare up at the inside of the brass chandelier. Three lightbulbs are missing. I've never noticed, have never looked right up into the spider's belly of the chandelier. I lie here imagining Charlie lying on the futon in his uptown apartment watching his X-rated movies. I think about calling him. Maybe we could have phone sex. The one time we did this we both fell asleep. I woke up hours later to a dead phone.

Except for inspired occasions, it's boring to masturbate and sometimes I even fall asleep in the middle, just drift away because I can't be bothered with myself anymore. Women's magazines always suggest that you work up to "pleasuring yourself" by drawing a hot bath with scented oils, lighting candles and pouring yourself a glass of wine to get in the mood. Who does this?

Charlie doesn't know it, but in the first month of our nearly ten-month relationship I duplicated his apartment keys. He asked me to move the car one morning and I had trouble finding a spot. I drove around and around the same two blocks, kept passing the bodega where we usually buy the paper. Each time I drove around the block, I saw a sign in the window that I'd never noticed before that said, WE MAKE KEYS. The next few times I circled by, it jumped out at me like a neon I READ PALMS sign. I watched as the guy behind the counter smoothed off the keys, the grinder shooting sparks. I added them to my key chain, mingling them with my own. I wasn't planning to use the keys, I just liked knowing I had them.

Perhaps he planned on sharing the videos with me? Certainly I bought the vibrator with its attachments for scalp and foot massage imagining the games we would play together, the way he would touch it to me as though holding two loose electric wires together, the way I would jolt and we would laugh. We would experiment. Together we would watch Tara at the gym with her bruised plum bottom and the way she took two penises into her mouth. Wasn't it incredible? Wasn't it grotesque? We would lie together in bed and watch. We would channel-surf, do pay-per-view. But this hasn't happened. Charlie doesn't know about my vibrator, and he doesn't know that I know about the videos, watch them when he isn't there, the same way I go through his desk and read letters from his ex-girlfriend and skim phone bills, listening for his key in the door. I've already planned an escape route. Is this how trust is built?

The first time I ever used the keys to get into Charlie's apartment, I stayed twenty minutes. The only thing I did was make a cup of coffee. I measured the coffee carefully, as though the sound of the sifting grains was too loud. I drank the coffee looking out the bedroom window, standing a little back. The silence rushed at me. I heard a dish break in a nearby apartment, muffled as though it was wrapped in a blanket. I kept lifting my nose into the air, trying to smell him. I washed the cup under a tiny trickle of water and polished it dry, wiped out the sink with paper towels, shoved them into my bag. I let myself out of the apartment, sweat trickling down toward my waistband.

The first wisdom I learned from a women's magazine was when I was a teenager. It said that a woman should always wear a smile so that men will wonder what she is smiling about and want to meet her in order to find out her secret. You never had to admit that you didn't really have a secret at all. I practiced this on the street, smiling randomly at passing strangers. They looked at me, puzzled, then looked away. Also at the magazine's suggestion, I tried imagining that there was a green light inside my forehead informing men that I was available and ready to go. But instead of an eager and beckoning suffusion of green, all I could envision inside my head was an old-fashioned stoplight dangling at an intersection, changing from green to yellow to red.

I become April for my amusement and protection, and also to entertain Charlie. We're driving along the highway and suddenly she bursts forth fully formed, begins tossing her head from side to side as though she's having a fit. She kneads my breasts with both hands, violently wrinkling my blouse. She purses my mouth the way they all do, Tara and Cherise and Jasmine, sticking both fore-fingers in my mouth to wet them and then placing the tip of each finger on each one of my breasts and saying *h-s-s-s-s-t,* as though putting out sparks. "Be April," Charlie will sometimes say to me now. I'm actually a little worried that I'll suddenly out of the blue say, "Fuck me with your big, hard cock, sailor" (from *Shore Leave*), while Charlie and I are making love, but I try hard not to let on that I've stolen some of my inspiration from his videos. My mate-rial in bed is, on the whole, my own.

Charlie wants to introduce April to a few of his friends because he thinks she's so funny. This seems a little too borderline, like jumping out of a cake at a stag party. I don't think I'll ever do it, but I imagine having dinner with his friends and drinking wine and April suddenly taking over, popping her cork like an after-dinner bottle of champagne.

I've been pretending to be April more often lately, even when I'm not with Charlie. The other day I made her slip through the turnstile in the subway after it devoured my token. She's definitely the one who stuck her tongue out at the guy in the token booth when he yelled after me; then she gave him the finger.

April often takes over when Charlie wants to watch.

"Just ignore me," Charlie says, leaning back with his hands behind his head, the same pose he adopts when he's watching basketball.

"No fair," I say. "You won't do it for me."

I wonder if Charlie knows that I do it differently when I'm alone; thanks to April, his ends up being a prettier show.

The first time a man asked me to touch myself so that he could watch, I didn't understand what he wanted me to do. As I tried to snuggle into him, he pulled away from me and patiently picked up my hand as though it was a dog's paw and plopped it down on my lower body.

"Pretend I'm not here," he kept saying.

Charlie leaves a message on my answering machine. "Hi, I'm just lying around polishing my rocket. I wish you were here."

Is this what men want?

I'm alone tonight. I've not yet turned out the light and have fallen asleep sitting up, propped against the headboard with three pillows behind me, head lolling down to my chest, holding a mug of tea. I no longer watch the late news. Murders become extremely personal when you sleep alone. I've sometimes fallen asleep like this for hours: lights blazing, shades wide open, until I startle awake and look around guiltily, caught by no one at all. Tonight, lukewarm tea spilling down my chest wakes me with a start. I change my wet nightgown, wander into the kitchen and eat a banana, dip it into a jar of raspberry jam. I try eating the banana the way April would, licking the jam from down near the peel and working my way up. The jam stains the banana a faded blood color and makes the strings stand out. I pour a small bowl of Grape Nuts and slice the banana on top and pour milk and stand there in the dark eating the cereal, looking out my kitchen window at the fire escape. I often do this in the middle of the night.

One night I start to call him, using the actual number keys, not autodial the way I usually do, and end up hanging up in the ominous silence between the last digit and the first ring. In the dark, I rummage in the drawer of my captain's bed. It's not there. I remember how I had awakened that morning and realized that I could feel my insides, my intestines and reproductive organs, all twisted up and knotted. My body was waiting for something normal. I took the vibrator from the drawer, briskly coiled the cord around its body, and marched it down to the basement, buried it at the bottom of a box of retired appliances: an electric carving knife, hot rollers, a Crock-Pot, all wrapped in newspaper.

Samantha has had a vibrator forever. Whenever I'm feeling guilty or upset about my addiction I call her for reassurance. I tell her about the peculiar cramps I get the next morning. "It's a life-line," she says. "I wouldn't live without one. Give it to me to keep. Get a safe deposit box." After I talk with her, the cramps always disappear.

In three minutes I've made the round trip to the basement and I'm back in bed, the piled shadowy basement a damp cement smell in my nose. In the dark, I plug it in and reach below the sheets in search of the spot, indented and familiar, soft as Italian shoe leather. I find it and nestle the head of the machine in there, expel the air from my lungs, feel my stomach go flat, my pelvic girdle curve up and wait. I think of Charlie for a moment, then fast forward to blank. In seconds, my body is tensed and pointed, heading down the narrow slope of the luge. My abdomen arches and buckles and heaps into a mound, a highway in an earthquake. It isn't right. It isn't natural. This affair is monstrous.

I fall asleep instantly.

I long for tenderness and sometimes I get it. I lie in bed in the half-dark, staring at the back of Charlie's neck. I will him to wake, to turn over and reach for me. He mumbles and gives a loud rumbling snore that stops abruptly midway, then he turns over and flings his leg over mine. The weight is at first comforting, then annoying. I pull my leg free. *Kiss my neck,* I think, staring into his sleeping face. *Wake up and kiss my neck.* I turn away from him again. I touch the back of my neck with my own fingers, feel his hot breath on my hand. Then I feel his lips. He presses his mouth to the back of my neck, right at the top of my spine, exactly as I wished for, as though he has actually heard me, though he never wakes up.

I know a lot of women, most women maybe, like to be the little spoon in the spooning position, the one who gets to be on the inside, the demitasse to his soup spoon, but I find, at least with Charlie, that I like to be the big spoon, the one behind. Not that I feel so strong and protective. I just like being at his back, pressing against his back, breathing in his neck, my arm around his chest. It reminds me of when I was learning to swim, holding on to an air mattress with one arm and paddling with the other, moving in slow circles, trying not to think of what lay below the surface.

I think I'm in love with Charlie, but I can't always tell. I think he's in love with me, but sometimes I'm not sure. The other night I burst into tears in the middle of making love, big hiccupy sobs so that I couldn't breathe. April never cries. She sits on top and pulls her hair back and gets this long-horizon stare. She comes fast and businesslike, falls asleep quickly afterwards. I always cry during sex, always thought that all women cry during sex, but Charlie still seems surprised.

"Why are you crying?" he asks, slowing down.

"I don't know," I say. He slows down even more, stops completely. "No, don't," I say, and push him right back in.

One night Charlie flips me upside down so that my face is pressed into the bed and I can't see him. He hauls me up into a wheelbarrow position and enters me from behind, steering me with my thighs. I keep turning around to look up at him.

"I love you," he says down the slope of my back as though to reassure me that we know each other. I turn back and press my face into the mattress. He's bucking up and down inside me, twisting a little, hurting me. I can tell he won't be able to stop, even if I ask him to. He collapses on top of me and I feel his will and strength ebb out over my head in a rush of air. I'm crushed under his weight, but I don't mind.

Later, I ask him if he enjoys it when he hurts me.

"Of course not," he says.

"Liar," I say.

"Happy? Comfortable? Safe?" Charlie's standard before-sleep questionnaire.

"Yes," I say, deciding, as usual, to believe that all of these things are true.

I've learned how to pick up the messages on Charlie's answering machine. It's easy to do. My heart beats the same way as when I'm searching in his closet. I hear his familiar, unsuspecting message that drags a little when he says his name as though the tape is being held back, and then the faint sound of a car horn from five floors down, right before he says "after the tone." I enter his code, standard AT&T, retrievable by anyone. The same guy who talks on my machine tells me, "You have three new messages." The tape rewinds. There's a call from his mother, two hang-ups. I strain to hear beyond the robotic "Please hang up, there appears to be a receiver off the hook, please hang up and try your call again." April calls Charlie again and leaves a message. *"Yes, YES, YEEEESSSS,"* she's saying as the machine cuts her off. I call back a third time to remind Charlie to bring milk and toilet paper when he comes over.

Samantha loaned me this book on self-deception that has a chapter on women faking orgasms. Basically, it says that women who do this are telling the ultimate lie about their bodies. I recently started pretending with Charlie, and I'm not sure why. I always used to let him know where I stood and when things were starting to happen. He said I give the most complicated instructions in bed of any woman he's known. But lately I've kept the information to myself. I'm guarding the road map. I don't want his questions and I don't want to have to explain myself. I'm mad that he doesn't seem to notice the difference.

Charlie has always liked oral sex in the car. He likes dipping into the passenger side, but prefers it done to him while he's driving in the fast lane, on highways. I tell him this is too dangerous. We both end up undoing our seat belts.

"What if we hit a pothole and I bite you," I say.

In the bobbing headlights and changing shadows on the driver's door, Charlie's head looms over me, his eyes wide open and young, his breathing torrential. I lose track of where I am. I get lost in the smells of his clothes and pubic hair and the old apple and coffee carton smell of the car. We usually don't finish this way. We get just so far and then he tells me to stop and I straighten up in my seat and look out my window, pink-nosed, interrupted, sad.

"I want to be inside you," he says in this thick, ultra-sincere voice. This is less about wanting to do something for me than it is that I think he gets frightened when he comes this way, with cars speeding at him in every direction, bridges and tollbooths looming up. After we park, he usually wants to grapple around the gearshift and the steering wheel under the streetlight. I complain that I want to go upstairs and do something more grown-up. We go upstairs, and, of course, we fight and I hug the wall all night.

Dead to the world, Charlie is lying here in my bed. I get up and go into the bathroom and shut the door and turn on the hot and the cold taps in the sink, then sit on the cold closed toilet seat and play with myself in a desultory fashion half thinking about something else, flipping through fantasies and discarding them like cards on an old Rolodex. I hate it when Charlie leaves me this way. A women's magazine would tell me to go and wake him up and discuss it, and then persevere until he's made me come. I've always been scared to wake people up. Once I woke Charlie and he sat up and looked at me blankly. He didn't know who I was. He made a sound deep in his chest. I grabbed him and held him tightly. I could feel his heart beating like a small animal's. I crawled down his body with my mouth, trying to coax him back, but he pushed me away. He was asleep the next instant.

In a flash of inspiration, I grab my new electric toothbrush from its holder and give myself a quick buzz with the back side of the toothbrush outside my nightgown, jump and quake in an automatic way, then feel immediately depressed and start to shiver because I realize how cold I am. I will never do this again. Turning on the light, I brush my teeth and look at myself for about half a minute in the mirror thinking that I look pretty: flushed, feverish, bright-eyed, too bad there's no one to see. I turn off the light and go back to bed and press right up against Charlie's back.

"Safe, comfortable, happy," he mumbles.

I find the video *Night Dreams* on sale for $6.99, not in my neighborhood. The cover shows a blond nurse with a stethoscope around her neck. A woman has been experiencing intense sexual dreams in her sleep. A doctor and a nurse place electrodes on the woman's inner thighs, which are then hooked up to a screen so that they can monitor her night disturbances. They suddenly see themselves appear on the screen and realize that they're inside her dream. The nurse stares at the doctor, finally pulls her hair out of her bun, takes off her glasses. She looks a little like April. He unbuttons his white coat. There's a scene with ice cubes. I find myself in a hardware store looking for an ice cube tray that makes moon-shaped ones.

I leave the video in Charlie's Timberland box one day, stopped right before this scene. It reminds me of when my mother used to place books open on my bed for me to search out the inspirational passages. I'm not sure what I want him to learn, although April seems to know. I throw away his old ice cube trays which are cracked and make drinks taste like onion powder, and replace them with the new moon-shaped ones.

A few days later I go to his apartment and use my keys to let myself in. Before I open his front door, I look up and down the hall as I always do and then slip quickly inside. Dragging my chair over, I pull down the Timberland box. I climb down and push *Night Dreams* into the VCR. The tape isn't where I'd stopped it, but has been rewound to the beginning. In a panic, I fast forward through the whole video using the remote, half expecting Charlie to suddenly appear on the screen wearing a white doctor's coat, his erection sticking out between the buttons. I stop at a few scenes that I remember and huddle under his afghan, turned away from the neighbors, feeling sweaty and aroused. Finally, I fast forward to the snow at the end and leave the tape sticking out of the VCR. The sleeve with a picture of the nurse, her breasts catapulting out of her uniform, is sitting on the living room floor. I leave it there.

Before I go, I look for one of Charlie's dirty T-shirts, and find one crumpled, half-lying under the bed. I sniff desperately at both armpits. The sweat seems sharp and foreign to me, enough to make my eyes sting. I smell effort and excitement and possible betrayal. I lie down on Charlie's side of the bed and bury my face in his pillow. After a few moments I lift slightly and spit into it, a thick projectile. We always argue about pillows. Charlie thinks he'll suffocate with his face in goose down. I imagine him going to bed that night, feeling the mysterious damp spot under his cheek, pulling back his head and staring down at it in the dark.

The only really useful thing I ever read in a women's magazine was a tip on how to curb credit card spending. For months I kept my Visa card frozen in a Ziploc bag until an emergency made me take it out of the freezer, dump it in hot water and pop it out of its protective iceberg. By then it had expired.

I buy a box of large freezer bags. I use the vibrator one last time, standing in my living room, braced and determined, not holding on to anything. My knees give way in the middle and I sag halfway to the floor with the majestic violence of my orgasm. Filling a bag with warm water at the kitchen sink, I submerge the vibrator headfirst and hold it underwater, waiting for it to stop breathing. I push the cord down into the water, but it coils back up at me. I squeeze out the last of the air from the bag with my fingers. Before sealing the final inch, I slide in Charlie's keys, and watch as they crowd up at the white plastic zipper as though seeking air. Opening the freezer door, I lay the bag neatly in the cleared out space in the middle of the freezer and stand there breathing in the billowing smoke. I feel like I've just sent my lover into deep space.

Every time I think about yanking the vibrator out of the freezer and defrosting it under the hot tap, flipping it out of its mold like a gun-shaped popsicle, I remember the empty shelf in Charlie's apartment. The videos have disappeared, and so has the Timberland box. Maybe we finally share something.

I keep waiting for Charlie to mention them. Secretly, when he's in the bathroom or out at the store, I look everywhere for the videos: underneath towels, in the medicine cabinet, even in the old-fashioned side cupboard attached to his oven with the mouse droppings and the crumbs, but they've vanished.

"Drink?" Charlie says, holding out the bottle. He's been rummaging around in my freezer the way he always does. We've just come back from the movies. The vibrator is now propped casually between a box of eggplant parmigiana and an organic chicken pot pie. It already has freezer burn. He's flipped right past it and grabbed the small bottle of Absolut just behind it.

"We should go to bed," I say, taking the bottle and looking past his shoulder at the looming shapes in the freezer. If this was a horror movie, they'd be body parts. I splash vodka carelessly over the coffee ice cream I've spooned into a teacup and enjoy the sweet, stinging sensation on my gums.

When Charlie leaves the next morning, I open the freezer. The vibrator looks entombed, a sea snake suspended in Arctic ice, the plug frozen coyly away from the body. I wrestle the bag from its resting place and rub it with the sleeve of my bathrobe. I take out the chicken pot pie to defrost for supper. I have coffee and a piece of buttered toast with honey, staring at where the vibrator sits smoking on a plate in the middle of the kitchen table like a piece of moon rock. Filling a basin with hot water, I hold the bag underwater until the ice begins to break up. I slip Charlie's apartment key into my bathrobe pocket. I put the chicken pot pie in the microwave to defrost. I dry the vibrator carefully with a dish towel, and plug it in slowly. April is laughing.

BACK RUBS

I USED TO LIE IN BED, WAITING FOR MY FATHER TO COME upstairs and give me a back rub. He did this almost every night, except when he had a meeting at church on Sundays.

My father gave the best back rubs. He pulled the sheet down around my waist and my nightgown up around my neck. With my head turned sideways, I could see myself in the long mirror on the outside of my closet door. I could see what was under the bed, sometimes a clump of dust, or a shoe turned over at a funny angle. (I wouldn't do anything about rescuing what was under the bed right then, just remind myself to do it later.) My arms were down at my sides, my palms curled upward.

He rubbed my back very lightly with the tips of his fingers so that I could hardly feel them. His hand went from the top of my neck, down to my waist where the sheets and blankets were bunched, then across from side to side and then down along my sides, but not underneath where my chest was pressed against the sheets. This was the map of my back he used. Right at that place along my sides where he stopped, it sometimes tickled more, but he didn't go past that place. I didn't want him to, but at the same time I held my breath when he got there. Tickling along my ribs was the best. Also, when he stroked around and around in circles that started out big and then got smaller and smaller until there was a tiny little spot right in the center of my back and his fingers were so light (and barely there) that my skin prickled. I was usually half asleep by then, and could feel the wetness under my face on the pillow where I'd drooled.

He always ended the back rub by counting the knobs of my spine, the vertebrae, he called them. He started at the top of my neck and counted down out loud, stopping at each one and rubbing it around and around in place for a second with the tip of his finger, so that I really felt the knob shape. He counted them, never missing one, until he reached the base of my spine. "How many?" I always asked. "Just the right number," he answered. Then he pulled my nightgown down.

My mother's back rubs weren't very good and she didn't give them too often. She would come in wearing her apron, which she was always forgetting to take off after doing the dishes. She wouldn't bother pulling the sheet down or pushing my nightgown up, but would just put her hands underneath and rummage around. They were very fast and impatient; you could tell her mind was on other things. She'd whisk over my back really quickly with the hard pads of her fingers that were coarsened by tiny cracks from gardening and polishing the teapot and pressing down on the frets of her viola. It was like being tickled by a rough broom. And all too soon I'd feel the covers being pulled up around my neck and my mother kissing my cheek good night. I always wondered if my parents gave back rubs to each other. I tried to imagine my mother with her nightgown around her neck. I tried to imagine my father counting her vertebrae. I wondered if he kissed her back afterwards.

He gets mad at me when I don't take my nightgown off, but I get cold. He never gets cold, even when he's naked. I tell him I'll take it off when we get going, when my blood gets going and I get warm, but he doesn't like waiting so long. When he starts giving me a back rub I'm all covered in goose bumps and my skin feels papery and breakable. I'm lying under a bright pool of light from the lamp by the bed and I worry that my skin looks blue.

He starts rubbing my back. His back rubs are too hard. He scrunches my skin, bunching it up in fistfuls like he's washing clothes then wringing them out. I don't know how to teach him. I feel my skin getting red under his twisting hands. Every once in a while he leans down and kisses my neck and then trails over and starts nuzzling my ear. I move my head slightly, away from his mouth and the heat of his breath. I know that he'll try to kiss my mouth next, sliding his tongue in from the side. I don't want him to. He knows I like back rubs to be separate. First a back rub, and then sex. He knows that, but he doesn't believe me. Back rubs turn him on. He won't believe me that for me they're something different. I turn my head away.

He straddles me, then lies down, covering my back with his chest. He keeps massaging my shoulders, bringing them up around my ears and down again in big circular motions, crouching low as though he's doing the breaststroke on my back. He starts riding me up and down, posting, up off the saddle and down again. I know he wants to fuck me this way.

His hands touch the sides of my breasts. I feel them flattened out and bulging to the sides a little, taut and swollen, painful, like they've been bitten by insects. He pats the sides of my breasts as though he's trying to open a cupboard, as though I'm going to lift myself up off the bed just to let his hands in there. I keep my chest and nose pressed against the bed. I don't want him there yet. I can't breathe. I turn sideways and am surprised to see the bare wall. I always expect to see a mirror, the white reflection of my face, shadowy shapes under the bed.

Still straddling me, he pushes off from my back as if from a springboard, then climbs off. He stands next to the bed. I turn my face to the sheet again, feel it smooth and cool on my cheek. I don't know what he's going to do next.

I want him to sit down next to me on the bed and start again, very slowly, breathing life back into me. I want the tips of his fingers to burn into my back. Right now, the room should be dark, with only a shaft of light coming through the door across the bed. My nightgown is as it should be, up around my neck, but he should be dressed and wearing a watch on his right wrist.

My two sisters and I are sitting in our "train formation," the three of us facing sideways on the sofa so that we are looking at each other's backs. We are sitting in the living room. The afternoon sun is wintry, slanting across the floor in panes of light onto three empty tea cups, a tray with a teapot, an empty plate that held cookies, and a small pitcher of milk. We've pulled our clothes away from our shoulders and necks. I've unbuttoned the front of my shirt so that only the very bottom button is done up. This holds my shirt on at my hips, but allows it to drape off my shoulders and way down my back. My bra is undone, my breasts loose underneath the cups, which have collapsed together in front.

I like to have the very bottom of my back massaged, below my waist, right where my buttocks begin, and this makes it easier for my sisters to reach. Our backs are all similar, straight and white with freckles on the shoulders. My sisters' backs always seem thin to me when I touch them, almost scrawny, and I wonder whether my back feels as insubstantial as theirs do under my hands.

We usually give back rubs within the first hours of a visit to my parents' house, or a visit to each other's homes. My older sister's husband seems to understand and smiles tolerantly at us as we gather our shirts up at our necks when he passes by, although he is ticklish and can't imagine how we enjoy it. My younger sister's boyfriend finds our behavior strange and perverted, an excuse not to have sex. He becomes jealous, banging pots in the kitchen until he storms out of the apartment. With this sister, we tend to give back rubs elsewhere, or when he is not there to comment.

In our train of three, one person receives but does not give a back rub. After fifteen to twenty minutes, we reverse positions so that the nonparticipant is giving one, which means that one of us gets a back rub twice. We keep track of this in an informal way and make sure that the same person isn't favored each time.

We have never really discussed whether this is something unusual that we do. We are not, otherwise, a family that touches a great deal. In fact, small birdlike hugs of the shoulders and air kisses are the custom. I pull away from my father when we greet each other so that our bodies don't touch.

I am at the back of the train today, the caboose. My younger sister sits at the front, the engine, her hands in her lap, idle. We give back rubs without oil, the slight dryness of our wintry skins shedding dust into the air. We don't speak. I stare into my older sister's back, feeling pity at the harsh red streaks I create, the tired slack of her shoulders as they droop down in relaxation, the constellations of freckles inelegantly dotting her shoulders. A sigh and another sigh. We communicate front to back.

As we begin the final circles, the light rubdown with the fingertips that signals a warning of the end, we hear footsteps on the stairs. Our fingers stop, just briefly, not quite frozen, but arrested in motion, and then continue in their light circles. There is the slightest adjustment of our draped-open clothing, not with hands and buttons, but with shrugs and shifting of our shoulders and upper arms, a token decency.

Our father stands in the doorway wearing his slippers, his hair upright from his nap.

We three sisters, the engine, the middle car and the caboose all look up. Our fingers don't stop. It is from him that we have learned our art.

"Hi, Daddy," we say. He is somewhat deaf now and doesn't seem to hear us. He looks at us and appears about to speak. He raises a hand toward us, his three grown daughters, our clothes in disarray. He half waves, then turns and walks away.

We continue the sad close of our ritual, the fingernails trailing up the sides, the feather-light circular movements around and around. We look behind our shoulders at each other, once, twice, slightly defensive, a suggestion of guilt. We lift our fingertips and pause, then finish with a brisk brushing off, of sadness or grief, or the talc of our collective dander.

We straighten our clothes and button our shirts. My younger sister pours the last half-inch of cold tea into her cup and takes a sip.

·   ·   ·

I know there is something trapped inside my back.

We are lying in bed having one of those awkward discussions about erogenous zones.

"My back," I say.

He's silent.

"Well, it is and it isn't," I say, embarrassed.

He turns me over and I feel him survey the wide flat bony field. He is lost without hills, points and valleys, the usual markers. He studies my back as though it is a chessboard. He plans his first move.

"Where?" he asks.

"Anywhere," I say. "The middle, up and down my spine." It is already hopeless.

His touch is tentative, as though I have asked him to blindfold, bind and beat me.

"Here?" he asks, a doctor prodding and palpating with his fingertips to find the exact spot for an injection.

"Fine," I say, giving up.

He lowers his mouth as though to a minefield and plants a small kiss in the exact bull's eye of my back, leaving his fingers there until his lips meet them.

His mouth stays, a soft and sucking leech.

I wait.

Bravely, his mouth roams and climbs the rocky face of my shoulder blade.

"Bite me," I command.

His mouth stops. I feel him opening his lips tentatively as though taking a bite of a strange new cheese. He bites down, softly.

"Harder," I say. "It doesn't hurt, you can bite me harder."

I feel an urgent chewing on my shoulder, and then coolness as the air hits the spit. He's given up.

"Thank you," I say.

I turn over and we continue, front to front.

I find his erogenous zones, standards, with ease.

The thing inside my back waits, trapped.

The room is soft and warm, dark as an incubator. She has left me, closing the door behind her without a sound as though the tiniest click might send me running. I take off my clothes quickly, piling them on a chair, and climb up onto the high narrow table. The mattress always astounds me, at once stern and hard, soft and yielding.

I lie on my stomach and fit my face into the padded brace at the head of the table that will carry the weight of my head for the next hour, funnel the rivers from my nose and mouth. I pull the top sheet up over my legs, leaving my back bare, and wait.

I don't turn around when she walks in. I hear only the sounds of her breathing, her palms rubbing together, as she stands next to the table. The strokes on my back are long and fluid with scented oil. Her two hands slide up and down the cage of my ribs as though on runners, stronger and stronger. I imagine her palms, darkening to crimson with the heat.

On the fifth upward stroke, my tears start, as though squeezed from a cracked tube of paint.

The thing inside my back groans and awakens.

My breathing is clogged and muffled. I turn my head to the side and close my eyes. She pulls the sheet up over my back and tucks it under my shoulders. She rubs her hands up and down my back one last time over the sheet, and then stops, leaving both hands there for a moment. I pray for them to stay.

She tiptoes toward the door and shuts it silently behind her. I lie very still, my breathing shallow, reluctant to sit up, to climb off the table, to dress, to reenter my life. For now, my back is as empty and clean as a new wooden box.

I didn't know it would be the last time.

It was soon after my twelfth birthday and I had begun to grow breasts, tiny swellings that barely pushed out my undershirt. I ignored them. Perhaps I knew that they would interfere.

After I'd said my prayers, my mother left the room and stood out in the hall talking to my father. In the middle of talking, she suddenly looked up into the darkened bedroom, saw me watching, and closed the door.

A minute later, my father opened the door and walked in and sat down on my bed. He sat down stiffly, right on the very edge. I could feel him almost falling off, as though he only planned to stay for a moment. I had already prepared myself, lowering the sheet to my waist and pulling my nightgown up around my neck, my skin gathering goose bumps.

Slowly, so lightly I could hardly feel it, he placed both hands, the very tips of his fingers, on my back, a pianist positioning for a performance. In the mirror, I could see them hanging down from his wrists.

His touch was so fleeting, his fingers hardly grazed my skin. He was tickling the air. I raised my back slightly, humping up, trying to make contact with his fingers. (Perhaps he didn't realize.) His hand pulled away when it met my back, up and down again, bounding. This was a new game. I didn't like it.

I shifted slightly, trying to urge his hand onto my sides, off the safe plateau of my back, but they stayed firmly on top.

Finally, he made a cross on my back, top to bottom, side to side, skimming my skin with one finger. I knew it was almost over. It had been so short this time.

He began the counting at the top of my spine, his touch finally firm again, rubbing each knob around and around. I turned away from the mirror and stretched out my neck so that my spine would be very straight, correct. He counted my vertebrae slowly, out loud.

I didn't want to ask the question. If I didn't ask, it wouldn't be over. I lay very still, my head buried in my pillow. He pulled my nightgown down and the sheet up around my ears. He leaned down and put his lips close to my ear. I could hear the dark gold whisper of his watch.

"How many?" he asked.

"I don't know," I mumbled into the pillow.

He sat for a minute or two and then he got up and left. He never came to my room again.

I dream about lifting my father's blue pajama top. His skin is so thin now that it wrinkles like white tissue paper. His shoulder blades jut out like the wings of a newborn bird.

Pouring rosemary oil into one palm, I rub my hands together briskly to warm them until they glisten. I run my hands down the center of his back, top to bottom, side to side An oily cross gleams in the half-light. I trace circles round and around his back with my fingertips. His face is pressed into the pillow where I once struggled to breathe.

Beginning at the base of his neck, I move down the bony range of his spine, counting each knob, massaging it round and around until I reach the end, not missing one.

EYES

I KNOW DR. MULLHAUSER IS JEALOUS OF OTHER MEN. I mention being attracted to the young Puerto Rican guy who works in the Korean market downstairs. Dr. Mullhauser clears his throat. I tell him how his eyes follow me around the store and how, when I'm standing at the counter, they stay zeroed in on me while he's putting lids on the coffee cups and bagging stuff. I'm sure he's practiced this technique on a lot of the women who come in for coffee and cat litter and donuts. Sometimes in the morning I apply eye makeup for just these few seconds of entrapment. We're taught to draw smudgy charcoal rings around our eyes, to lure, to pull in. We're trained to look deeply into someone's eyes. Women have been doing this throughout time, and yet Dr. Mullhauser doesn't get it.

I've been trying to explain to him about this problem I've been having lately with making eye contact. I get paid to have men look at me. I hoard their gazes. I pluck out the hot, dark centers. Somewhere in the world, they cut out men's eyes for looking the wrong way at a woman. Those wrong looks keep me alive.

But something's changed lately.

* * *

This is how I started this job: One day I'm serving drinks to
men at small tables. The next thing I know, Jack, the bouncer,
picks me up, puts me on the runway and takes my tray. So I dance.
It's surprising how quickly you get used to your breasts falling
loose in public.

Spanky Lee, another exotic dancer at the Peekaboo Lounge,
told me to pick out one guy at the bar and stare right into his eyes
and not take mine away for a second, so I wouldn't lose my concentration. Inhabiting strangers' eyes is something I'm good at. I
chose a man at the bar in an expensive gray suit. I held his stare.
For a moment it felt safe, locked in. But his eyes were hungry, too
raw for entry. I found myself turning away. So I made up this rule.
Now I never look past the hands holding glasses as I skim by in
high patent leather pumps.

I tell Dr. Mullhauser that I no longer know how to look into
men's eyes. He nods his head and tucks it to the side and gives me
a wink. As I talk, I practice holding his pupils with mine, but all
around those dark pinpoints his face starts to move and change. I
force my eyes to refocus. With the X-ray vision you develop after
years of therapy, I settle on the dough wedged between his two
front teeth, a tiny flour and water giveaway of the life he leads
upstairs with a wife and child and a basket filled with fresh bagels.

"Why do you feel the need to make eye contact?" Dr.
Mullhauser asks in a tactful murmur.

"What do you mean?" My heart begins the familiar thudding.
I focus on the expensive fake Oriental rug and the sleek digital
clock placed at just the right angle on the uncluttered desk. "Don't
you ever look at your wife?"

"How do you feel about men looking at you?" He stares at me, his eyes pale and steady behind his clear plastic glasses.

"I want them to look at me at work. Obviously. If they don't I get fired."

"How does it make you feel? Do you enjoy it?"

His stomach gurgles from across the room with a faraway plumbing sound. Two therapized adults politely ignore it.

"Do you find pleasure in it?"

Sometimes, I imagine Dr. Mullhauser sitting alone at the gleaming wood runway bar at the Peekaboo Lounge. I see him ordering a brandy in a balloon goblet. Knocking his pipe into the ashtray and noticing, with clinical detachment, the big-busted torso etched in the glass. He doesn't miss his mouth with his glass like the others. His stare focuses beyond me as I stand over him, playing with my G-string. I pull it away from my body and execute a few of the deep back bends that have earned me my stage name, Candy Cane. It is this movement, sweet and pretzel perfect, that invites bills to be stuffed and poked, folded or crumpled, deep into the scarlet satin pouch over my pubis, shaved smooth as a young girl's. I learned how to do this on the lawn when I was six, arched over the sprinkler, in front of my father's movie camera.

"How do you feel when I look at you?"

I know what he's pushing for, but I don't submit. I refuse to tell him my dreams. I refuse to tell him how often I imagine my father sitting at the bar watching me. How I see his eyes turning red, even though he doesn't drink. How they shift and dart around my body, never rising above my neck. How I see them there together, my father and Dr. Mullhauser, sipping drinks, talking, the way men do, about other things, never realizing it's me there above them, dancing.

.   .   .

I looked deeply into my father's eyes only once. It was a Saturday afternoon at the lab. My father is a medical researcher, a man who makes eye contact with squiggly, live things on slides. Things that might end up changing the world if they were to move this way, rather than that. When I was a kid he taught me to stare into the eyepiece of a microscope with both eyes open, an alien act that seemed similar to trying to breathe under water. It scared me to learn that your pupils weren't round, hard and coldly touchable, like marbles, but small black holes, actual openings. I worried that things would find their way inside and be free to roam around through those tiny portholes.

That afternoon I was playing with the microscope. Carefully smearing a daub of the culture on a slide, I covered it with a slip of thinnest glass and gently inserted it under the lens. I moved the two small pieces that held it in place so as not to disturb what looked like a greasy thumbprint of Vaseline. All morning I stared into the microscope until the muscles behind my eyes felt strained and hot.

When I finally looked up, my father had pulled his swivel desk chair right up next to me. I jumped.

"What do you see?"

He was holding his glasses in one hand. The skin around his eyes looked pink and tender and I could see the tiny black holes at the very center of his eyes. I had the feeling that he'd been staring at me for a long time. I couldn't remember ever seeing him with his glasses off. He looked old, and at the same time very young, like the brownish photographs of him as a boy propped on my mother's bureau, with his pale naked face, blinking and exposed, under the sun. I wanted to reach up and press the white puffs of skin in the curved glasses shape under his eyes.

"Squiggly things that look like threads, moving around," I mumbled, looking quickly back down into the microscope at the mucousy world full of life-forms reaching up for me. Losing focus, I shifted my eyes slightly to the right until I could see just the toe of his shoe and the cuff of his pants near my feet. I continued pressing my right eye tightly into the eyepiece of the microscope and squeezed the left one shut so that my father's feet disappeared. When I looked up, he was over on the other side of the laboratory looking in one of his books, his back to me. He'd put his glasses back on.

I pull the last two Kleenexes out of the box without looking and half rise from my chair, holding the balled-up soggy ones in my lap so they won't fall on the rug.

Unlike my last therapist, Dr. Mullhauser is extremely tidy. When it rains or snows, he lays down plastic strips, crisscrossing them in a complicated flight pattern, one leading to the bathroom, another to his office door. A separate, slightly thicker piece of plastic the shape of a place mat sits squarely in front of the large armchair reserved for patients. I sit there and talk, watching him watch the water from my shoes form a pool on the plastic.

"Are you trying to get me to say I'm attracted to you?" I say. "Well, I'm not. I don't know why you keep trying to get me to say that."

Dr. Mullhauser places his long white fingers together so the tips meet exactly. His forefingers just touch his lower lip. "I'm not trying to get you to say anything."

I'm actually not in the least attracted to him. My mind shuts down when I reach his neckline where the few reddish hairs curl up out of his shirt. I imagine that he leaves on his glasses and watch when he makes love to his wife between psychological emergencies. I hear him making high, whimpering sounds that are over quickly. I try to shut this out. You're supposed to be able to tell your therapist things like that, but you can't really. They'll only take it out on you.

I tell him this: Last night, Jack, with his huge barrel chest in a crisp billowing white shirt and hair sluiced back in a swirl of licorice candy pulled me against him until I could feel the gun under his armpit. Jack doesn't understand why I work there and it's too hard explaining that neither do I. Jack assures me in his grainy slow voice that I'm a good dancer. As good, he says, as Spanky Lee, who closes her routine by kneeling on all fours in the center of the runway and slapping each buttock over and over with fingers tipped in black nail polish.

Jack doesn't understand about having problems with eye contact. On the first night we made love, he took off his jacket and his shoulder holster cut through the snowy white shirt like a puzzle piece. When he came over to the bed, I gathered the material in my fists and buried my face in it.

"Hey, watch it. Mascara never comes out." He pulled my head away and peered up at my face to get at my eyes. His were velvety brown and eerily warm.

"You should know," I said, finding his shirt front again, feeling one of the small pearl buttons on his dress shirt between my lips, behind it the hard stomach. "All those women crying on your shoulder."

Jack stared right into my eyes the whole time we were making love, even though we were still almost strangers. When I tried turning away, he took my chin between his thumb and forefinger and brought my face back and found my eyes, not roughly, but insistently, as though this was the way it had to be. He wouldn't let me keep them closed. When I tried, he kept stroking my eyelids very gently with the tip of his finger, first one, then the other, until I finally opened them. He stared right into the very centers of my eyes. This is very different than men looking at you from far away.

Dr. Mullhauser listens, his eyes polite. I know he can't believe I sleep with a man who carries a gun. He opens his side desk drawer and takes out another box of Kleenex and carefully pokes at the perforated strip. He starts to wheel his chair toward me with small jerking movements. My nose is clogged and the air finds only a small whistling passage. Taking the Kleenex box from him, I carefully place it on the end table at just the angle I know he likes. I lean back slowly.

"You're too close," I say.

He reaches out slowly toward my forearm with the slightest hesitation as though I'm a bird with a broken wing.

"How does that make you feel?"

I sit, completely still, looking down at the rug. Finally, he backs off. I go on talking.

I tell him about last night. I was supposed to go on in ten minutes. Jack came over to me and told me Spanky Lee wanted to see me. She was sitting on the toilet in the small bathroom off the dressing room, her costume a pool of black sequins in the middle of the floor. She was naked except for red satin high heels. I breathed in a few floating fibers from the black feather boa curled by her feet like a soft, shedded skin.

"It's happening again," she said. "I can't go." I pictured her on

the runway, body arched, hair sweeping the floor, bladder
stretched and aching under her feather fans.

She wouldn't look at me. I kneeled in front of her and tried
taking her hands. They were freezing. She grabbed for me, encir-
cling my wrists so that her long black fingernails met in jagged
clusters. I made comforting clucking sounds.

"Do you want me to run the water?"

She nodded and let go of my wrists. I rubbed at the chilled
white bracelets of skin. I went over to the sink. It was stained like
pink sandstone with layers of makeup. I opened both faucets until
the water just hit the edge of the drain, making a soothing indoor
waterfall sound. I filled a plastic cup with lukewarm water. She
held her wrists out in front of her, veins up, and I poured the water
over them in a slow steady stream until her face crumpled in relief.
She reached behind her and flushed the toilet, covering the sound.
She looked up at me. We stared at each other and listened as the
toilet tank filled. Tears trembled in the corners of her eyes but
didn't fall. She's good at crying without ruining her face.

Dr. Mullhauser is staring at me strangely. We've been sitting
here for forty-three minutes by his digital clock. My face feels raw
and puffy. I'm thinking about cool water. I'm thinking about how
tired I am of the sound Kleenexes make when you pull them out
of the box, raspy and soft at the same time. He's got a new brand
this week. Pink, scented. They make my nose itch. I wonder if his
wife bought them on sale.

"I want to leave therapy."

There's a long silence. He's cleaning his glasses. He holds them
up to the window. Rubs a little more. Puts them back on.

"I really don't think that's a good idea." He pulls back in the high clinician pose he adopts when he talks about sex, face backed up, eyelids lowered for combat.

"Why?" I ask calmly.

He starts inching toward me again in his chair, his eyes growing bigger behind his glasses as he gets closer.

"Stay and let us work this out together."

"Work what out together?"

"Your anger about your father. Why you need to undress in front of men for money."

"Oh, please."

"What does that mean?"

"It means, spare me."

I close my eyes and push back hard into the couch.

"What are you feeling? Why do you pull away?"

I get up and grab my bag which sits half open at my feet. I have to step over his brown Hush Puppies to get past him. He's wearing thin black banker's socks. I yank open the office door and cross the hall to the bathroom. I leave the door open. It looks like a motel bathroom. Cleaner than home, with a bland wash of yellow. I never leave anything in the wastebasket here. When I have my period, I bury the cardboard tube in my bag and take it with me. I've never told him this.

My nose is swollen and rejects makeup. My eyelids are oozy and delicate, but I manage to draw kohl lines and smudge them properly with my finger. Through the open office and bathroom doors I can see Dr. Mullhauser watching me in the mirror. It's one of those sliding bathroom mirrors that you have to almost lift off the track to open noiselessly. I opened it once. There was nothing inside but a man's small black comb. I combed my hair.

Dr. Mullhauser's phone rings. He lets his machine pick up. He usually doesn't do this. He usually answers. We have fights about this. I think he's worried about what I'll do when his back is turned.

I don't meet his eyes in the mirror, although I feel him staring at me in the glass. I outline my lips with a dark burgundy pencil, scratching first at the wood to find the tip. Then I fill in the outline with lipstick. The line is steady, perfectly formed. I am strangely, distantly surprised by this.

I turn off the light and close the bathroom door quietly behind me. Dr. Mullhauser has taken off his glasses and is leaning forward, his elbows resting on his knees. He looks up at me in the office doorway. He strokes the row of pens in their plastic protector in his front shirt pocket, swiveling the chair back and forth slightly with an imperceptible motion of his hips. His eyes have a pinkish cast, and he looks tired. He blinks rapidly, not quite able to keep his gaze on me.

"So," he says. I stare at him and don't say anything.

The phone rings. His eyes shift a little off mine. I know he wants to reach for it. He lets the machine pick up again. "How did that make you feel?" he will want to ask me next session.

Just before the door clicks shut behind me, I remember my umbrella. It's been there for months, sitting next to the coatrack at the bottom of a long black tube with wire mesh on top. I left it there, with its broken metal webbing, for weather emergencies that might blow up while I'm in my session. I hesitate for a minute with my foot in the door, then slip it out and watch as the door shuts.

I can hear him talking on the phone.

Tonight I take off all my clothes, except for my G-string.
Tonight I break my own rule.

The man I pick out is sitting at the bar by himself drinking a martini. I zero in on his eyes and hold them as I dance. He can't look down. I see him feel for his drink like a blind man. I'm in control again.

Another man at the bar throws his glass high in the air with a whoop and hits one of the spotlights, showering the runway with glass, leaving it with the glittering splendor of a car accident. I don't want to stop. Jack signals me to keep going. I close my eyes, losing my place, and continue to dance, feeling the glass crunch and powder under my pumps. A couple of the men at the bar begin to chant. I arch back, skimming the floor in a back bend, my hair and fingertips lightly touching glass. "Can-dy-Cane, Can-dy-Cane," they shout.

Upright again, a pulse bangs in my head. I stretch my eyes wide, feeling skin pull around bone. Inside, my body opens in a liquid channel down to my G-string, the open hole of a smooth-skinned black olive, briny, secret, dark. I keep dancing, pulling in the dusty brightness of the one remaining spotlight. From the shadows behind the bar, Jack's eyes glitter into mine. I see the center of my father's eyes, small and bright and still, the wise beady knowing of a lizard.

I look recklessly from one man to the next along the bar, not pausing at the hands around the drinks. Upside down again, my heart beats in my belly, narrowed to a curved bridge. The faces change and jumble in a childhood game of mixing face parts. From upside down, a man's tongue curves at me, a thick meaty arch. The end flicks up, double jointed, and waggles.

I flip upright again. The blood drains. I have this feeling inside that is empty and bursting at the same time. Any second now I will scream and rip off my G-string, pull it out, fast and harsh, hideously, from where it is squirreled between my legs, tear at it with my teeth, swing it above my head like a damp, glittering lariat and hurl it out into the darkness, at the raised glowing faces of men.

I touch my hands to my face. I'm so dizzy. I curtsy low, and the money down there shifts, cool and crisp, next to my body.

"Pick out one guy and eat out his eyes," I hear Spanky Lee's voice. "It's the only way to keep your balance."

PARKING LOT

I DON'T KNOW WHAT I'M DOING OUT HERE. I DON'T EVEN drive anymore. I learned over twenty years ago, in another lifetime. Now I'm trying to figure out how to park a Jeep Grand Cherokee in one of those angled spots that you find only in the suburbs. I think I went down the parking lot the wrong way. I'm not even sure if there is a right and wrong way to drive in a parking lot. These are the things, the information, the contact points, that you lose when you live in the city for a long time. My skills are different. I know how to slip unobtrusively into the next subway car when someone across from me starts playing with a knife.

I've gone and done what they tell you never, ever to do. I've given up my one-bedroom rent-stabilized five-floor walk-up in Manhattan and moved out of the city. Not to a pretty country house with a quaint staircase and a claw-foot tub and a place to grow herbs in the backyard, but to the suburbs. The burbs. I came from something like this, but I left it a long time ago, vowing never to come back.

There's something about the stillness out here that has nothing to do with peace and quiet, but more to do with things that are hidden. The streets are so wide and quiet and the windows have a blank look, as though no one has ever leaned out on their elbows and looked up and down the street. The doorbells have a sitcom ding-dong that echoes rooms and rooms away. None of this is in the least like my city apartment, which had a practical front door with a dead bolt, a police lock and a chain, and a long harsh buzzer that pizza deliverymen liked to lean on. People in the suburbs are always taking care of their property. Cutting stuff up with circular saws inside their garages. Shoveling snow or watering the lawn or washing the car or hosing out large garbage cans or standing at the end of their driveways with their hands on their hips surveying what looks to me like nothing.

Basically, I'm here because I met someone who asked me to live with him, and I finally decided that I had to say yes in order to get the word "ambivalent" out of the circuitry of my brain. Just saying or hearing it now sets up a strange buzzing inside my head, maybe it's the "biv" part of the word, so that I actually see a hive with bees swarming outside it, unable to go in or out. This picture is probably scientifically incorrect, because I'm sure that bees, although they seem to swarm in an indecisive cloud, know exactly what they are doing at every moment; I've read that a beeline is actually a precise zigzag course not unlike that of ships when menaced by submarines.

Ambivalent is one of those words that's terribly overused these days, thanks to all the therapists, and twelve-step programs and women's magazine articles about commitment. People no longer just say that they don't know what they want. They say "I'm ambivalent." This word has crossed my own lips countless times. It now gives me an intense feeling of boredom and irritation when I say it, and yet it seems so much the right word for a certain kind of mental state. The worst time to say it is directly to someone. Saying it in a conversation to a stranger about someone you're involved with isn't so bad. "I'm ambivalent about the relationship," can slip by unnoticed. What's tragic is when you're forced to look someone in the eyes whom you're trying to be in love with and say, "I feel ambivalent about you," even though it's as near as you can get to the truth.

Jim lives close to his mother, who has a bad hip and walks with canes indoors and a walker outside. I think she would like him to live with her, and I sometimes wonder if he is seriously considering this. He hovers over her with anxious tenderness, smoothing invisible ripples from rugs in her path. I wonder if this is my future as well, and see myself walking next to her in the dead quiet of this suburban town, staring down at her balding head and then up at all the still, closed houses and back down at her hands clawed around the handles of the walker.

In the last two weeks I have given up my apartment, quit my job, found a home for my cat (Jim is allergic to dander), sold much of my furniture, dismembered many of my plants, wrapped my dishes in newspaper and put them in storage and moved into Jim's apartment with only two suitcases of clothes and a box of my "things," as I keep calling them. So far, I've only unpacked a pair of carved wooden candlesticks that have different colors still embedded around the holes, rose and teal and cinnamon wax run together from various dinner parties over the years.

The carpet in Jim's condo is wide and green and plush. He keeps a Dustbuster in the hall closet propped against his golf clubs, and he's always taking it out for a quick "pick 'em up." Jim manages a wholesale lumber business, and he usually arrives home covered in a film of wood dust and gives himself a vacuum. At the strangest times I will suddenly get the sharp, fresh taste of plywood at the back of my tongue.

On the whole, I'm a fan of old oak floors and area rugs. For years I've been sweeping bare wood floors, sweeping corners, sweeping rugs, sweeping city dust and small black things that could possibly be mouse droppings, but I don't look too closely; these are the details you'd rather not know when you live in a building with a lot of other people. I have this feeling that I might dissolve into a helpless babyish mess out here, unable to get up off the rug.

This morning I arranged my candlesticks on Jim's dining room table. They looked awkward and vulnerable, too weathered and nut brown. They need my long wooden table to sit on. Before I left the city, I visited my banquet table that I bought at a sidewalk sale, now entombed in a long, low storage space in Queens. Jim's table is glass on a wrought-iron frame, the kind you can look through when you're eating and see your lap and your feet and what the other person's hands are doing under the table. I like to sit with one foot tucked under myself and take my shoes off, and I often end up undoing my jeans or skirt after I eat. This doesn't seem possible at a table like this. Jim also serves food on glass plates so that you can see down through the clear space between the potato and the vegetable in a disturbing visual through-line to the floor.

I feel like I'm camping out in someone else's place. There's a whole suburban vocabulary here that I don't yet know. Jim calls his stove "the range." I miss my greasy black gas burners. I'm worried about dropping his wedding flatware down the garbage disposal.

Last night he made pigs in a blanket using the same Pillsbury Crescent Rolls recipe that my sister and I used to make when we were teenagers. He peeled off the silver wrapper and carefully lined up the marker on the cardboard tube with the counter, then raised it high above his head and slammed it down so hard that the dough bulged out like fat splitting out of skin. Turning to me, he brandished it playfully.

"I surrender," I mumbled through a mouthful of wine. A few minutes later he beckoned me over and together we watched through the little square window in the oven door as the dough puffed up around the baby hot dogs.

When I say "the condo" I sound like someone else, so in a way I can say it quite easily. "I'll meet you back at the condo later," I said this morning to Jim, standing with the keys to the Jeep in one hand. I've added the keys to his condo and his Jeep Cherokee to my key ring, attached on a little separate ring of their own. I'm unable to throw out keys, so that I have sets from old lovers' apartments, bathroom keys from former jobs, even an old-fashioned wrought-iron one that looks like it should open the door to the Secret Garden. I like its weight. They hang in connected circles from the ignition like a magic trick.

Now that I've parked, I don't want to get out of the car. I'm worried about losing the Jeep, coming out of the Stop And Shop with my cart and not being able to find it. It's higher than a lot of other cars, but it's not the only one here. I don't see any numbers indicating which row I'm in, like in airport parking lots. You just have to remember. From where I'm sitting I can see three vehicles that look just like this one, high and forest green with the same kind of roof rack. I see myself wandering up and down the rows of cars with my cart, trying to jam my key into resistant keyholes until the parking lot empties out and it's midnight and Jim's lone Jeep Cherokee is standing there, accusingly.

I find a piece of paper in the bottom of my bag and a pen and balance my address book against the steering wheel so I can lean on it

to write. I used to stay in the car when my mother went shopping so
that I could read. She never seemed to worry about this, never told
me to lock the doors or not to speak to strangers. I once masturbated
in a big parking lot just like this one, in broad daylight in the backseat of my parents' car while they were inside shopping. This was
soon after I'd learned how, and the jolting, compulsive novelty had
not yet worn off. It was almost dusk, with the eerie unsettled qual-
ity of an early Sunday evening permeated with school dread. I had
my coat draped over me, and I kept myself very still, making a tent
of my underpants with the same hand. My parents came through
the doors and started heading back to the car, wheeling a cart with
a turquoise hamper sticking out of a brown paper shopping bag. My
father pushed the cart and my mother rested her hand on the side as
though she didn't trust him to guide it in the right direction. I kept
my eyes on them as my hand moved. They weren't talking to each
other. I knew I couldn't stop until I'd finished, and I knew I had to
finish before they got to the car. I did, just as they approached the
door. I could see the middle section of my father's coat on the
driver's side and my mother's on the passenger side, their buttons
and bulky wool bellies pressed up against the glass.

"Aren't you cold like that," my mother asked, not paying any
attention to what she was saying. My coat still covering me, I
snaked an arm out from underneath and pushed my fingers into
the lattice of the new hamper.

"Any ideas for supper?" my mother asked. No one said anything. My father started the car. We'd had waffles with creamed
chicken every Sunday supper for as long as I could remember.
This aberrant meal, with its confusion of syrup swirling into
cream sauce, epitomized the Sunday feeling for me, uneasy and
hopeless. I studied the creases on the back of my father's neck
above his coat collar. He glanced at me once in the rearview

mirror. I looked down at my right hand in my lap, now bearing the scars from the hamper along with the marks of my zipper where my open fly had pressed.

"How about waffles with creamed chicken," said my mother.

Everyone's bringing in shopping carts from outside, wrenching them from an angular silvery caterpillar in front of the store. I'm usually more comfortable with a basket that I can hang over my arm. There's more mobility that way; they're easier to abandon unobtrusively in an empty aisle when the contents don't add up to anything that makes sense: a jumble of marinated peppers in jars, cleaning products with miniature companion samples hanging from them and six bunches of bagged carrots on special for a dollar, nothing for dinner.

Jim took me shopping here for the first time last week. His ex-wife lives in the neighborhood, and he seemed to develop a strange electromagnetic field the moment we drove into the parking lot, repelling intimacy. When I remarked on this, he shrugged, moved ahead of me and began intently comparing the prices on cans of tuna fish. I went to the produce and began bagging an assortment of lettuces while he lingered for a long time at the beginning of the aisle, studying the price markers on the fruit with a frown. Finally, he came over holding a bag of wizened McIntosh apples, which he set carefully in the baby seat of the cart.

"Let's make a pie," he said hopefully, eyeing my voluptuous bags of organic Red Leaf, Boston and double heads of Bibb. He leaned over and kissed me. He thinks I'm extravagant and that he'll train me out of it.

"Those are the wrong apples," I said. As we looked at each other, the misters emitted a fine, cool spray and the chorus of bees rose and subsided.

．　　．　　．

"Let's cohabitate," Jim said to me three months after we met. We were sitting in a restaurant. I was busy creating a miniature city on the tablecloth with my knife and a maze of bread crumbs. The houses had no windows, I noticed. These houses were no place anyone would want to live. I began studiously making bay windows by twisting the base of my wineglass in the crumb walls.

"I hardly know you, you hardly know me," I said, realizing I sounded like song lyrics.

"It's the fastest way to get to know someone," he said filling my wineglass a little too full. This was a decent red, and I now know that half-full is the right amount. I've also learned that you should hold a wineglass by the stem, the only way to avoid covering your whole glass in a web of smudgy, guilty-looking fingerprints and transforming your wine into vinegar with the heat of your hand. For years I've meant to take a wine-tasting course, but have never done it and keep buying wine sheepishly and unknowledgeably, attracted to the tiny brush strokes of the vineyard on the label, or getting a feeling, the way one might at the racetrack, about a name or an age, and taking a chance.

"Either you hate each other after two weeks, or two months, and you don't waste time dating for five years, or else it works out," Jim said, looking sincere. I already recognized the look. I studied his sweater. Jagged snowflakes and animals with boxy, Nordic antlers marched across the modest tundra of his chest. The flower smell of his aftershave wafted down into the balloon of my glass and up my nose. His ex-wife hovered.

"I already know that you don't like to talk until you've had coffee in the morning," he said with a small smile. "Isn't that good for starters?"

I sometimes wonder about the theory that says people who are attracted to ambivalence are actually ambivalent themselves.

With two fingers, I picked up my glass by the stem and, looking into Jim's eyes, clinked it against his.

"Cheers," I said.

"Tables," he said, looking pleased.

The swarm of bees banked sharply to the left and dive-bombed for the bushes.

I was back in the city for the first time yesterday. I stood on the subway platform at Grand Central waiting for the crosstown shuttle and stared at a man who was wedged in the middle of the car in a business suit holding up a folded paper but not reading it, like an ad for city burnout. He looked right at me and then smiled. I smiled back and shrugged and then realized he had no idea that I had already gotten in and then out again of three trains because they were too crowded, and that I didn't have to act so apologetic. I thought maybe he wanted to pick me up. Maybe he would be waiting for me in Times Square, posted by a pillar pretending to watch one of the Peruvian street groups angelically playing wooden flutes, but really waiting to spot me and stop me and talk to me. Maybe he had a house with a garbage disposal so powerful it could grind up shinbones, and a two-car garage that you could open from a block away with a magic button attached to the sun visor. The doors would open and swallow me, driving his BMW, the moment I turned into the drive. Maybe I would never see Jim again.

The subway doors kept opening and closing, opening and closing, until everyone had pulled their raincoats and the straps of their pocketbooks and knapsacks in out of the way. I stood on the platform watching the people inside the car look back out at me as though they were in an aquarium—dumb, gill-breathing fish. Then the train pulled out. The man watched me only until I wasn't in his line of vision anymore.

I walked back through the tunnel to Grand Central and went upstairs and bought myself some stockings on sale, four pairs for ten dollars. By that time I figured the rush hour was safely over and the trains thinned out, so I went back down to Grand Central and got on a train leaving the city, a real train, not a subway, which actually felt all right, and arrived home to Jim's (our) condo, where I microwaved some leftover Kung Pao Chicken and in the two minutes that it was heating tried on a pair of my new stockings with my black patent leather high heels that I only wear like this parading around at home, and then walked around eating the Chinese food, which was filled with the usual frightening microwave cold pockets, looking at my legs in the mirrors that seem to be behind every door.

Then I felt guilty because I'd eaten without Jim, automatically, because I was hungry, like a thoughtless, ambivalent single person who has no mate or loved one to think about but comes home and eats pathetic meals standing up, practically choking and needs to swallow the same mouthful twice because they're eating so fast. I considered purging, which I've never done before, but decided not to. It was definitely not good to close out my second week of living in the suburbs with Jim by exhibiting the early warnings signs of an eating disorder. "I'm just not hungry, honey," I practiced saying out loud. Then, "I was so hungry, honey, I just had to eat." Instead, I got into bed and decided to be asleep when he got home.

My shopping list is longer than the back of the scrap of paper I'm using so I turn it over. It's an old creased D'Agostino register receipt and I stare down at the items on the list feeling nostalgic and weepy. Scot TP, Evergreen Hummus, Alladin Pita, Land O

Lakes Unsalted Butter, Pudding Brownie Mix, d-Con Mouse Prufe II, Frozfruit Bars. A whole life swims before me. I remember that night, I whisper out loud, as though watching a home movie in a darkened room. I see the plastic tub of extra-garlic hummus that I bought by mistake, the garlic so strong it raised rough bumps on the back of my tongue, but I ate it anyway, scooping gobs of it up with a shovel of pita. I drank two glasses of chardonnay that night, or was it three, the wine tasting sweet and sour, landing on all the wrong places in my mouth, but hitting my pleasure center in a straight shot. I needed this in order to fumigate my apartment, to load the mousetraps with pale D'Agostino-brand Swiss cheese, wedging it under the fake bright yellow plastic gadget that kept snapping down on my fingers. Next, I dumped piles of mouse poison into tiny espresso saucers, finally finding a use for them since I could never figure out how to operate my espresso machine. The mounds looked so pretty, I worried that I might wander into the bathroom or next to the fridge in the night and think, in one of those floating, irrational dream states, that the beautiful piles of rough turquoise gems were something to eat.

After setting the traps and pouring the poison and finishing the hummus and recorking the wine when there was about one-third of the bottle left—respectable, not quite twelve-step material—I once again took out the flannel nightgown that I had several times already that season spread out on my dining room table. I stood over it, scissors opened and poised at the edge of the hem, prepared to cut and rip it into dust rags. Instead, I closed the scissors, both hands in a fist around the blades as though muzzling an animal, and put the scissors back in the top drawer of my desk, and slipped the nightgown over my head.

•　　•　　•

Jim loves paper products, one of his plan-for-a-hurricane qualities that I find endearing. When I'm by myself for the first time in the apartment I go into the kitchen and start opening cupboards. His food cupboard is pretty ordinary, in fact, on the sparse, bachelor side. A few weird items that only men would buy, cans of Dinty Moore Beef Stew and Corned Beef Hash. I always feel sad when I see men in supermarkets and they have their carts filled with hopeful-looking items like that, hearty meals in cans, Hungry Man frozen dinners, which you know are really awful processed lumps of baby food in little molded metal compartments. I imagine these men, the kind of men I so often want to go home with, wheeling around the aisles and falling in love, attracted by the name of a product or a picture of a home-cooked meal. I've been taken in this way myself, have looked at pictures and had a vision and bought something and gotten it home and been embarrassed and disappointed. Frozen dinners always make me feel like that, even the good ones. There's something so shrunken and naked about the food when you first take off the wrapper, as though each item has been swimming way too long and become beached and flash frozen somewhere. And single portion servings are so single. In fact, they're usually not even enough for one. That's why when I see big workmen with dusty hair and bits of building materials hanging off their clothes at the grocery store right after work I feel like asking them if they'd like me to come home and cook them supper. Of course I don't, because, as I tell myself, these guys are probably perfectly happy with their six-packs and their grub and The Game on the boob tube. I'm the one who's feeling lonely and pathetically single-serving tonight and projecting all over the place.

Clearly, Jim has no problem stocking toilet paper. He keeps this along with paper towels and Handi-Wipes, everything papery and shreddable, in a long wide cupboard that stretches above the others. I have to climb on a kitchen chair to look inside. He has two eight-packs of toilet paper in there, one white Cottonelle and another Scot in that pinkish beige color that I abhor. Maybe women have a harder time with this color because it's always tricking them and making them think they've miscalculated their periods. But it's a depressing color, not quite pink, not quite mushroom, and it can't possibly go with anyone's towels. Certainly not Jim's. He goes in for bath sheets, which I like in concept but have trouble with in reality, mostly because they're so heavy and awkward when they're damp. The first time I wrapped one around my head turban style after I'd washed my hair, it wrenched my neck back and I had to adjust the whole construction forward and then walk around carefully as though I was balancing a jug on my head. Also, they're solids, brown and black. I've decided that maybe these are towels he brought from another lifetime when he had a very manly bachelor apartment and his bathroom had lots of chrome fixtures, one of those zigzag spring-out shaving mirrors and track lighting, not peachy theatrical bulbs around an oval mirror that make you look startled and glowing, even first thing in the morning. I can't get used to the way we look together under these lights, standing at matching scalloped basins, wearing only towels. It's one of those moments when I get an unreal feeling and pieces of my old life float before me. I'll suddenly see myself sitting in a raised bathtub in the middle of my old kitchen while Mario, an old boyfriend, stands naked at the stove, eating tomato sauce from the pan with his fingers. All the windows are steamed and there's a slick of oil on the surface of the water and my newly washed hair smells of garlic. I keep staring at the radio and small lamp sitting on a table within arm's reach, thinking how easily they could land in the tub. I explain this to Mario and then we both start laughing hysterically and then he climbs in with me and squeezes up near the taps facing me and starts stirring the water between my knees with the wooden spoon.

Jim and I took a shower together for the first time the other evening. The shower has rippled glass doors that shut with a terminal magnetic click. Jim got in after me and pulled the door closed behind us. I kept angling myself to avoid his full inspection. Even though I've never met her, I keep picturing his wife's ass. I sidled around him under the showerhead, switching positions, so that my back was against the door, and then pushed the door open again, slowly to avoid the click, but Jim opened one eye even though he was in the middle of shampooing his hair. The streaming water made his chest hair look like a dog's, long and shaggy over his nipples, and a blob of spit mixed with the shampoo on his chin. He grinned.

"I get too hot," I said, feeling my breasts droop in the heat. I began soaping them vigorously to bring them back to life, not wanting to explain the way that closed shower stalls make me feel as though I'm in a gas chamber. He took me by the waist and pulled me directly under the spray with him. I gulped convulsively as though I'd swallowed half a heavily chlorinated pool. Our mouths tasted bland and watery together without the thickness of our sex in bed. I kept pulling back and wiping under my eyes, worried that mascara was running down my face.

The other day, looking for a can of Drāno because the toilet wasn't flushing very well, I found a few strange things in the cupboard under the bathroom sink, which makes me think there's been a woman around the condo more recently than Jim's letting on. I tend to overuse Drāno, have become too used to it the way people can get addicted to nasal sprays, to having passages

wooshed out and functioning swimmingly at all times. I decided
Jim's toilet was a little sluggish and could use a shot, even though
I know it's hard on the pipes. I figured this double-doored closet
under the sink was the logical place to keep Drāno, tucked away
in the back in case there are visiting pets or children, although that
doesn't ever seem to happen at Jim's place, which is a disappoint-
ment.

There was no Drāno, although I did find a pink plastic toilet
brush in its own special sheath, a stack of unused blue sponges, a
six-pack of Ivory soap, one of the bars already ripped out, and the
only really interesting thing, which was a long plastic box, similar
to a pencil box that I used to have in grade school, filled with
makeup. I took this out so that I could examine it more closely
because it's hard to see anything very well in pink light. I locked
the bathroom door first. There was a reddish brown Clinique eyebrow pencil, a lipstick, which I opened and tested on my hand, a
pinkish mauve shade that didn't seem to go very well with the eyebrow pencil, a tiny tube of Lancôme moisturizer, a few spongy
synthetic makeup remover pads, and a stringy piece of loofah, as
though someone had cut a narrow strip from an ordinary phallic
loofah in order to exfoliate some very small, specific area. I took all
of these out of the box and laid them side by side on the back of the
toilet and stared at them for a while and then put them all back in
the box and then back into the cupboard.

I poured more Drāno into the toilet than I should have, so that
the water in the bowl fizzed and exploded up at me, and I averted
my face just in time, the way they warn you to do in the instructions to save your eyes.

Whenever Jim and I get into conversations about his ex-wife, I
realize that we're treading on dangerous ground, but I can't help

guiding us there. I suppose I'm jealous of her, of the commitment they managed to make to each other for a while, even though half of the rest of the world has tried marriage and it's not as though anyone has a very good track record.

I've decided that the makeup must belong to her and that Jim can't bring himself to throw it away. I know she's a redhead, I've seen pictures of her with her tousleable bowl of copper curls against a variety of green collars, so the shade of eyebrow pencil fits. Last weekend when Jim was picking up his mother for lunch at our place, I took out a photograph album that I'd spied on the bottom shelf of the bookcase in the living room. I was supposed to be fixing lunch, and I wasn't very far along in my preparations when they returned. Jim hovered behind his mother as she lurched into the kitchen on her walker like a demented cross-country skier wearing a witchy black coat with its collar turned up, ignoring me. Her eyes roved hungrily over the counters. He had both of his hands outstretched behind her.

"Been busy?" he asked me, sounding annoyed.

"Ready any minute," I singsonged, not looking at him. Already, I remembered as though it was my own history, the protective way he stood behind his wife throughout the album, under trees, next to tents, in front of the Taj Mahal and the Grand Canyon, his arm draped across her shoulder, and how she looked so confidently and openly back up at him. Jim isn't very tall, and I avoid wearing high heels, which I love, when I'm with him. I resent feeling so large and graceless, someone who will crash into things and have to find her own way back from humiliating errors in spatial judgment. I am, in principle, all for towering above a man in high heels. But whenever we're dressing to go out and I slip on a pair of sensible flats, I look over at him in the bathroom as he leans comfortably toward himself to shave and feel furious at him for taking away this option of easy femininity, to be able to totter back in a man's arms on my favorite pair of two-and-a-half-inch pumps, and be steadied.

All during lunch Jim and I watched his mother expectantly. He keeps a special phone book for her to sit on, the pages stuck together where she wipes her fingers. I was looking up local hairdressers one morning and had to cut the pages apart.

"How's your lunch, Ma?" Jim kept saying, looking over at me each time as though we shared something precious. Her canes lay crossed on the floor next to her like abandoned oars. Through the glass tabletop I watched as the crusts from her sandwich collected in the drooping net of her dress.

I've finished with the shopping list, which looks ridiculously long for only two of us, even though I haven't even thought about dinner yet. A cluster of people has congregated at a table set up right outside the entrance to the Stop And Shop. A big banner over the table like over a politician's booth reads "Spice up your life with Salsa, Mild, Medium or Hot." A high school–age girl wearing a bright red chef's apron and a high headdress shaped like a red chili pepper with a green cloth stem sticking out from the top of her head stands behind the booth handing out samples. She pokes both elbows out at her sides and puffs her cheeks as she struggles to open a bag of corn chips.

The first time I tasted salsa was on a New Year's Eve when I was thirteen. My parents, who didn't drink or believe in staying up until midnight to see the ball drop on TV, had taken to hosting a small celebration for the family at 9 P.M. We would sit around the dining room table under the bright overhead light, eating potato chips and dip or salted pretzels and glasses of Hawaiian Punch mixed with ginger ale, and take turns reminiscing constructively about the year past and ahead until 9:30, when my father made a toast. The festive air of the party derived from the fact that we drank out of small paper cups, and that we weren't normally allowed junk food.

With the sullen, jokey sarcasm only a miserable thirteen- and fifteen-year-old are capable of, my sister and I filled and refilled each other's glasses from the pitcher and kept raising them to each other in private, whispered toasts, "Here's to a zit-free year!" and "Happy Screw Year!"

My mother put the salsa away, saying we'd had enough, but at ten minutes to midnight my sister and I stole the half-full jar from the fridge and the remaining chips, neatly stored away in a plastic leftovers bowl, and took them up to the attic where we opened wide the one small window facing the city, which lay a dim, distant beacon in a glow of lights and pollution. We finished the chips off, toasting the frosty night air at the stroke of midnight, calculated by our identical Timex watches, with triangles of corn, dripping spicy red juice on the windowsill, amazed, as always, at the astonishing, deadening, absolute stillness of a New Year's Eve in the suburbs.

I have the urge, now, to jump out of the Jeep and join the throng in front of the table, to stand there and comment on the salsa, perhaps to engage in conversation with one of my new neighbors, to feel active and entitled and a part of this friendly, milling scene. But I don't. I sit there wondering how I'm going to be able to extract one of the carts and maneuver it into the store with all those people in the way. And what if Jim's wife were by sheer chance to saunter along as I stood there chatting, and dip a corn chip into the salsa and turn to me with a big smile and say, hello, who are you?

· · ·

Last night I insisted that we switch sides of the bed to sleep. Jim and I had landed on opposite sides after making love, and then because I suddenly became aware that he was uncomfortable, preparing to clamber back over me in the adult return to home base, I resisted. For me, the nighttime hiss of modern heating ducts, the big motel shapes of the credenza and the armoire, are still foreign suburban artifacts. I wanted him to experience this minor terror in transplantation.

I've already teased him about his ex-wife keeping his side of the bed empty for him across town, how, until anyone else fills it, which he is infuriatingly certain no one has, it remains his, an empty doghouse waiting for its master. He still has a key to her house, formerly theirs, a fact he rationalizes because of their as yet hopelessly intertwined "financial dealings," suspicious to me for two people who have been divorced for three years and share property but no children.

"Don't you think she still sleeps on *her* side of the bed?" I insist, unwilling to drop the bone.

"Probably," he says. "She likes to be close to the bathroom."

"And if you slept with her again, wouldn't you go right back to the same side?"

"Yes, I'm sure I would. But I'm not going to, so what does it matter?"

I sit up, shielding my naked breasts with crossed arms. "It's just that I don't have that," I say. "You have this backup plan all ready and waiting for you, an empty side of the bed with a bedside table and a reading lamp, and probably even your favorite books there. I don't have that." I'm crying, and getting stuffed up and I reach for the Kleenex box on my bedside table but it's empty. Meanwhile, Jim is rummaging under my pillow while I'm leaning forward and hands me two old Kleenexes, flattened into gnarled driftwood shapes that glow in the dark. I feel a surge of love for him, for knowing this about me, that I store Kleenexes away under pillows like a squirrel lining a nest. I blow my nose with a honk. "Seriously, don't you think you'll end up back with her?" I say.

"No, I don't," he says firmly. I feel ridiculous relief at this. And then he adds, "Unless you know something I don't know."

Sitting up again, on my knees this time, I blow my nose with a renewed fury, the mucus shooting through the tattered Kleenex into my hands. "Why do men always say things like that," I say. "Something that makes it clear they bear absolutely no responsibility for their emotional choices?"

"You're here with me in my bed, aren't you? Isn't that a choice?" Jim's voice is soft and calm. He's speaking to a mental patient.

I give a long exasperated sigh and flop dramatically over him onto my side of the bed, kneeing him in the stomach so that he makes a comical *oooomph* sound, and lie there on my back staring up at the ceiling, wishing I were home, remembering that this is home. I suddenly think of the way my cat used to lie on my chest and gaze into my eyes when I cried, pressing one paw passionately against my chin.

"Sure, Jim, anything you say, Jim."

Sighing in unison, we turn our backs to each other with a great show of pulling and rearranging the covers and lie in huffy cartoon poses for a while without saying anything. After a while, he turns around and starts rubbing my back.

. . .

The sun is shining through the windshield, directly on the driver's seat. I put the cap back on the pen, a new habit for me, but I get worried about ink leaking on Jim's pristine Jeep upholstery, and shove the list and the pen and the address book onto the dashboard, and then slump down on the seat and close my eyes. I like the height of the Jeep, the individual armless buckets of the seats, the way I feel as though I'm on safari, but safe. I decide I'm going to deliberately not think about shopping for a few minutes, allow the items to swim freely inside my brain, Zen-like, in hopes that the random list will miraculously transmogrify into tonight's dinner menu.

I'm feeling drowsy and sexy and warm when I remember that the Jeep's doors aren't locked. I bolt upright and start fiddling groggily with the master control panel, my heart beating fast. There's a strange, high-pitched buzzing in my ears. Somehow I push the right button and all four locks slam down in unison with that prison gate sound. My cornered rat response in the middle of this placid, trundle-through parking lot makes me feel incredibly lonely.

A kid in a yellow Stop And Shop jacket comes out of the store. He's wearing new black Converse high-tops and walks with a springy, wiry step as though there's no fat on his body keeping him earthbound. His hair is shaved all the way up to the bony part of his head, with a gelled wedge sprouting from the top, and he's frowning. Probably he has hickeys all over his neck.

He stops at an island of abandoned carts in the middle of the lot and steers one expertly into the back end of another, bumper car–style, until five carts are packed on. Eyes squinting in concentration, he backs them all up and takes a long looping left turn and heads toward the entrance, steering his load with awkward precision. He begins to jog and then to run between the rows of parked cars, and then with a flying leap, jumps onto the carts, his body stretched flat and lean along them, elbows tucked into his sides as though he's steering a toboggan. Gigantic sneakers dangle over the handlebar.

He's heading straight toward an elderly couple walking slowly on either side of a shopping cart. I moan and cover my eyes. When I finally dare to look, the kid is strolling into the Stop And Shop, his hands in his pockets. The carts are neatly parallel parked out front. The old man is fumbling with the keys on the passenger side of an old car while his wife keeps patting his overcoat, her fingers bent into a loving, arthritic semaphore on his back.

Jim's car phone rings, the sound sweetly trilling. I scramble frantically all over the Jeep trying to find it. Finally, I spy the phone hiding half under the passenger seat and dive for it, just as the ringing stops. I feel incredibly relieved. Jim and I have yet to establish our respective phone habits, as mundane and crucial as toothbrushing. He only learned last night that I like to read while I brush my teeth, undisturbed, my book propped between the faucet and the toothbrush holder, gathering tidemarks. I suspect that once the novelty of my telephone screening habits loses its sexy, scampery, us-against-the-world appeal, Jim will become impatient with me. We still haven't recorded a joint message on his answering machine. Over the years I've lived alone, some of my answering machine messages have been tiny works of art. Sometimes I spent hours finding the perfect measure and a half of music, running down and back up the four flights in my apartment building at midnight, dressed in my bathrobe, just to give my voice the right combination of breathiness and confidence.

The phone rings again. Either Jim's wife is calling, trying to catch him alone, or he's calling to find out where I am and what I'm doing. The prospect of either of these domestic dependencies scares me. I let it ring.

I have to go in and shop. I'm supposed to cook tonight. I know that if only I could make one really good meal at the condo, something peppery, oily, dark and so spicy that it would saturate the loveseat cushions with the smell of garlic for weeks—then I will begin to feel at home.

Ever since I've moved out of the city, I can't remember what it is that I cook. I do remember that I am a good cook. Apparently the recipe file box in my mind, the only place I ever really had one, spilled out on the expressway en route to the suburbs and left me with an empty box, devoid of even one simple pasta dish. The stove in the condo has burners made out of crinkly baked acrylic that look like glazed-over pastel potholders. One burner merges into the next with only a token gingerbready border under the glaze, a little like suburban backyards. How to cook properly when pans with slippery Teflon bottoms skitter indiscriminately into each other? Add to this boundary problem the fact that Jim has casually dropped several remarks about "burner maintenance." I am culinarily blocked.

More than once, I've wondered whether Jim would reconsider his commitment to cohabitation if he'd taken a quick peek at the greasy crawlspace beneath the top of my old city stove before I moved, a scabrous carbony wasteland lit by a pilot light that valiantly sputtered, occasionally dying under all my experimental acts of deglazing with everything from oyster sauce to 7 UP.

The phone rings again. This time I grab it before the end of the first ring.

"Hello," I say, in an assertive, already-been-shopping voice.

"Forget the shopping." Jim's voice sounds far away and excited. "Let's go into the city for dinner tonight."

I stare out over an acre of car roofs, hefting the connected key rings hanging from the ignition in my palm as though I'm weighing precious metals. The hive doors yawn wide.

"Too late," I say. "I already bought a leg of lamb." A menu is revealing itself to me, invisible ink held to a candle, something with mustard and garlic, maybe honey.

In the silence I imagine Jim rubbing the line between his eyes hard with one finger, reprogramming his life.

"So come on home," he says.

ME and MINE

MONDAY

I PRESS THE SNOOZE BUTTON DOWN FOR THE FOURTH, THE final, time and lie in bed staring at my digital clock. 6:52? Why such sadistic, odd-numbered snooze increments? I can't get out of bed until I know where my black skirt is. I envision it, beautifully ironed on a hanger. It may be either scrunched in the laundry cart or at the cleaners. Closing my eyes, I look again, one cold leg outside the covers.

I've developed a system for getting myself to my job so that only a small part of me knows what I'm actually doing, just enough to get myself dressed and on and off the subway, buy the paper, a large coffee and a bran muffin, take all of this to my desk, sit down, drink the coffee, surreptitiously read the paper, folded in eighths in my lap, finish the muffin, get rid of the crumbs, apply lipstick using my Christmas grab-bag mirror that I keep in the top drawer of my desk, go to the ladies' room where I continue to read for ten minutes in the far stall, careful not to rustle the paper too obviously so that one of the legal lickers will report me, then bury the newspaper in the wastebasket, wash the ink off my fingers, make my way back to my desk and log on to the network using my secret code before Dragon Lady comes by on a thinly disguised productivity check. The key to having a secret life in the office is to pretend that you take as long to do some things as the other secretaries do, while you're actually doing something else.

I sit facing forward, twisting my legs into a vine in the dark square box of space beneath my desk. This cuts off my circulation and will give me varicose veins. All good secretaries have varicose veins. My boss tosses a tape into my box as he passes by. He smells of androgynous cologne and coffee. Sometimes he has a white caking at the corners of his mouth. Antacids. I dread it when he stops to tell me something, to give me instructions. He presses his starched white shirt into the ledge in front of my desk, and beats his fingers. His cuffs are monogrammed and droop down his pale wrists.

"I need that yesterday," he says. I disappear into one of his pearlized buttons, right into the tiny holes where the thread loops.

The tape rewinding sounds like hysterical birds. To make sure that I'm not erasing it by mistake, I always listen as the tape rewinds. Once I erased a full side. There was a whirring silence. The red warning light was on, I noticed this at the end when the tape clicked, but I switched the machine off and turned it back on, pretending that it hadn't happened.

"This tape is blank," I said, standing at the door to his office dangling it between two fingers.

"That's impossible," he said, half-rising from his chair.

"It's completely blank." I shrugged. "There's nothing on it." He turned bright red and the baggy dog-jowl part of his face shook. He is a young man, prematurely middle-aged. His eyes got all greasy and pink, and he stared right into the centers of mine, putting a hex on me. I stared back.

"Do you have any idea what you've done?" he said.

His skin was all blotchy. I watched the spit fly from his mouth.

His wife watched us from an 8 × 10 photograph on his desk, an indifferent referee. I don't understand who the pictures are for. It's the angle I don't understand. Not facing Them, not fully facing the door or guest chair, but angled just enough in that direction as though an offer is being made. The frames are filigreed silver or gold, or beautiful polished oak. This is what I have, they say, and I can afford to package it right.

When he tapes at lunchtime, he chews in my ear and then swallows for a long time as though something is stuck. I try to tell by the sound of this chewing what he is eating. A bagel with cream cheese makes the words thick and sticky; a salami and provolone sandwich on a hard roll is mumbling, slimy with mayonnaise.

I listen to his taped voice all afternoon, imagining, as I type, stabbing his throat with the fine point of the bone-handled letter opener he keeps in his ebony desk caddy.

I rise and glide with purpose to the ladies' room. Choosing the far stall, I begin what I'd suddenly felt compelled to do while typing the table of contents for a loan agreement. Someone walks in. I stop, suspended, with blurring, radiant vision, as though a VCR has been paused, my insides beating wildly. I clear my throat, remove my finger from myself and spin the toilet paper roll a few turns, feigning enthusiasm, pretend that I am doing my business, that this takes some time. I check that my clothing is not draped exaggeratedly on the floor, to raise questions.

The person next to me, with the black leather pumps and the sepia stockings, is also taking a long time. We've gotten to know each other's treads, the knobby shape of our shoe lasts. I'm becoming impatient, losing my place on the climb.

"Is that you, Marie?" she says.

"No," I say.

"Are you sure?" she says.

I hope that a guilty smell is not coming from my stall. She is probably distracted by her own. Finally, I hear the sliding friction of her clothes, the snapping and popping of elastic on skin. She washes her hands for a long time, pulls two, three, five, paper towels from the dispenser. Her heels click on the tiles and then stop. Has the door closed yet? No, she must now be standing at the mirror, examining herself front and back, the rupture lurking beneath the skin on her chin, the pull of clothes across her behind. All of us do this, the secretaries, pick at our faces leaning close into the mirrors under the fluorescent lights. Then I am alone again.

Jellyish and light-headed, I walk back to my desk. My fingers on the keyboard feel thick, and for a few lines I misspell words. Still trembling, I finish the letter and ricochet through spell check, office pinball.

After I've taken the last cool, caramel sip of coffee and thrown the carton in my wastebasket, the first trash of the day, I mourn the passing of the event as if it's a death and think about it happening again the next morning and feel in that moment that I can't wait. I refuse to keep a mug at work, the office mug, the I Love My Boss mug, the Aetna Life Insurance mug, the bears in sex positions mug, to add to the tawdry ceramic mess in the kitchen sink. The others pile mugs in the kitchen sink, occasionally with magnificent mold sculptures, and sneak away, leaving them for the Cleaning Angel.

I do not need one more magnet that shows me that Mine has gone to St. Martin again. In my desk drawer lives a collection that will never see my refrigerator: a shellacked sand dollar, a miniature pink ceramic conch shell, a hula girl in a skimpy bra, a green lei and hips that swivel. The scene is clear to me. He's sitting in the airport with his wife, their daughter and the baby, surrounded by bags. Suddenly he groans. He rises and walks toward one of the airport shops and twirls the revolving display near the cash register two, three times quickly, then selects a magnet, pays for it, returns to where his wife and children sit. Half-pulling it from the bag, he shows it to his wife and they laugh together. As the baby reaches for it, he pokes it down into the side zipper pocket of his briefcase. He gives it to me on Monday morning still in its white paper bag with the register receipt inside. I thank him. "Nice tan," I say, staring at the piece of skin scaling off the tip of his nose. Later, I will make the right noises when I see the photographs of the baby eating sand.

Sometimes I have a bagel along with my cup of coffee, but never a real breakfast. We are not allowed to eat at our desks because of the smell. A bagel does not smell. Sometimes I buy an oversized cruller from the man in the coffee truck on the corner and it sits all morning long, a sugary phallus on the ledge of my computer immediately above my A drive, where I can easily take bites from it.

The clients must not smell food as they walk from the conference room past our desks to the elevator banks. They must be protected from the smells: bacon, eggs, home fries, toasted corn muffins with butter, Chicken McNuggets and especially Chinese food, which hangs in the air with the mothball pungency of damp wool coats.

I've worked out a method of eating at my desk so there is no smell. The food from the Korean salad bar downstairs comes in hard plastic cages with ribbed sides and an attached lid that fits perfectly onto the bottom when secured with a red rubber band. I pile food into the container indiscriminately so that Caesar salad ends up next to or on top of moussaka and hot wings become embedded in squares of red Jell-O. It is my theory that sea legs, the compressed strings of fish parts designed to simulate the texture of lobster, with their suspicious nail polish–red edgings almost the color of crabmeat, were invented for secretaries, to give us the illusion of luxury within the range of our budgets.

I tuck the food cage in the space between my computer and printer and look down into it, strategizing my next bite. When I am certain that no one is coming down the hall toward my desk, I carefully open the food cage, trying to muffle the lightning crack of the lid, then slip my plastic fork inside, down along the edge. Stabbing the piece of broccoli I have already decided on, I guide it out as though I'm performing microsurgery inside an incubator, close the lid quickly, then bring the piece to my mouth, meeting it halfway by bending down, hunched and furtive. I no longer notice the taste of preservatives.

What is this "new language" they're always talking about? They stand in clusters in front of desks in the middle of the hallways, obstructing people's movement around them, dark-suited rocks in the middle of a river. "I've created new language for the Agreement," Mine says to another. We call them Mine, even though we don't want them.

While I am here putting in my time, I try to learn something. I've grown attached to the words, the ones with long voluptuous vowel sounds and many syllables. *Exculpatory, jurisprudence, attornment. Reckless misconduct,* one of my favorites. I want to know the difference between *gross* and *ordinary negligence.* Are *incidental damages* really unimportant, *extraordinary remedies* something special? When I hear the word *plaintiff* I see a man with droopy spaniel eyes. I now know that the official word for ashes is *cremains.*

I go through a great many batteries each month. I now own two Eveready Charge Mans. One is plugged into the outlet under my desk at the office. Another is in my bedroom at home. I am always in the process of recharging a set of AA batteries for my Walkman and a set of AAA batteries for his tape recorder, which I borrow over the weekends and sometimes at night when I know he's finished taping for the day. He's careless with his tape recorder and leaves it in all kinds of strange places. I once found it balanced neatly inside an old drinking fountain down the hall, dried up as an ancient riverbed.

I always take out his batteries and tape and leave them in my top right-hand drawer in a special envelope and replace them with my own. Although he is in some ways absentminded, leave it to Mine to know exactly how many units of power are left in his batteries, even though the firm pays for them. I don't worry about the wear and tear on tapes. We have access to these in the supply room, but not to batteries. I do worry that he will rewind and replay a section and find my voice there instead of his.

When I am at home I sit in my bathtub and set the tape recorder on a folded washcloth on the corner ledge of my tub. It looks like a tiny stereo speaker sitting there, elfin and sweet. I lean

forward and pick it up, making sure that my hand is completely
dry, and then lie back in the tub so that my shoulders are underwater. I hold the tape recorder right in front of my mouth the way
he does. He makes a small circular stirring motion with his wrist
when he clicks it on and off, stalling for time. When he speaks, he
holds the microphone part right up to his mouth the way singers
do so that his lips are pressed against it. I always carefully clean
that part of the tape recorder before I use it, never after I use it,
although I do check that there are no lipstick marks on it. I like
knowing that the next morning he will be eating my germs.

Some of the legal words sound dirty to me. Because I have no
formal legal training, I have my own associations with these
words, definitions that mean something only to me. *Inter alia,* well
of course, sitting in the bathtub. And *per stirpes.* Whenever I'm
typing a Last Will and Testament and come across that term, I
can't help it, I see a woman with her feet in stirrups and her legs
spread wide open. *Intestate,* a man is lying naked in a coffin, his
erection sticking out above elaborate brass handles. *Litigious, cliti-
gious,* the list goes on. Sometimes when I'm using my vibrator,
these words run through my mind in a kind of humming rhythm,
all strung together. Right at the end I say out loud *in rem, in rem,
in rem,* almost chanting the words, like a Buddhist praying for
prosperity. Sometimes I think I should apply to law school.

At this moment in time, I have two IOAs (Inappropriate Office
Attractions) in my stable, an unusual state of affairs. For the past
three weeks my primary IOA has been Peach, the head of office
services, the only man in the office who doesn't wear a suit, but I'm
getting bored. He always smells of fruit lotion, which he stocks in
his desk drawer in a variety of tropical flavors, papaya, mango,

kiwi, all of which smell to me like my name for him. When I walk
into his office, he's always rubbing thick, custardy globs into his
hands and the back of his neck as he talks on the phone. This act
is not as girlish as it sounds. Peach is the felt-tip pen demigod. He's
also in charge of changing lightbulbs and carrying cartons of office
supplies around and around the corral. The office is laid out in a
big circle, with stalls where we sit. The only thing we don't do is
eat hay and whinny. The slight greasy sweat on Peach's face is a
rare exotic oil in this dry place. I want to touch it. He wears something on his hair that leaves it black and glistening smooth, the
strands neatly separated. He wears a necklace, a piece of iron
hanging from a black leather thong. At least five times a week, I
pretend I need to copy a document so that I have an excuse to go
to the Xerox room and stand near him and furtively breathe in his
fruit scent. IOAs must be kept secret.

Several times a day, I look up at the fluorescent lights behind
their checkerboard grid in the ceiling above my desk and feel like
I'm in an experiment. When one of the long tubes directly over my
desk burns out, the light is suddenly dim and soothing and full of
possibility. I ask Peach not to change it.

"I have to, man," he says, shrugging. He brings the ladder over
and sets it up right by my chair. He asks if I want to move and I
say no. Sitting next to the ladder, almost under it, I put one hand
out and hold on to the middle rung so that his leg is right by my
hand. I stretch out a finger so that it just touches his khaki pants
leg. He pulls the ceiling light grid down and lets it hang by a hinge
at one end. As he fits in the long fluorescent tube I stare up at his
chest flaring in ghostly outline beneath his shirt. Looking right
into the light, it feels as though I'm staring directly at an eclipse
and my eyes are going to burn out. Peach stares down at me, smil-

ing, snapping the grid back into place one-handed, without looking. I wheel back a little in my chair so that he can climb down.

Once a day he walks by my desk, stops and puts down the box
he's carrying, and comes around my desk and massages me really
hard, digging his fingers into the base of my neck and manipulat-
ing my shoulders this way and that. Goose bumps immediately
spring up on my arms and my nipples stand out.

"You're stiff, man," he says. "Like rocks." I blush and pull
away, lean over my computer to hide my face.

"Thanks," I say, trying to sound casual. "That's just what I
needed."

"Cool," he says, picking up the box.

Miss Born Again, typing across from me, looks up from her
computer and smirks. I start typing again, too, concentrating on
making my nipples soft. Peach and I have brushed past each other
before, passing in doorways, getting off the elevator. I've willed
these moments to happen, sometimes thinking about nothing else
all day. The second I step off the elevator and leave the building,
he vanishes from my mind. These are the curious parameters of an
Inappropriate Office Attraction.

*Plaintiff, after making an innocent misrepresentation, discovers
the truth yet thereafter silently allows another to act on the misrepresentation . . . though the original representation was true when
made . . .*

Every Monday morning a woman in a long black silk raincoat
and a trailing black chiffon scarf delivers a flower arrangement
to the magazine table in the reception area. This arrangement is
not top tier but not bottom either, a modest, moderately uncre-
ative design, often including statice and daisies. Sometimes I've

ridden up with Secondhand Rose in the elevator. She leans with her back pressed into the corner, the day's arrangement hiding her face in a jungle disguise. I'm jealous of her job, imagine a cool ferny back room, oversized canvas gloves, cutting shears, her head cocked as she pokes long-stemmed roses into wet green sponge. I want to inquire about an apprenticeship. I stole the florist's brochure from Call Girl's desk and now keep it in my bottom drawer. I like to take it out and look through the arrangements, most of which I now know by heart. I especially like Funerals Nos. 5 and 6. These are large tasteless displays with lots of phallic white lilies and satin ribbons. On Mondays I try to be in early so that I can rescue the few still-alive flowers from the previous week's bouquet and put them on my desk before she comes in. Secondhand Rose insists on taking away the old arrangement intact. I, in turn, insist on my right to take a few dying flowers, a principle akin to emptying the roll basket into your bag at a restaurant.

Months ago I picked out a sleek black vase with an obsidian gleam from the jumble in the cupboard of the office kitchen and keep it permanently on my desk for my drooping, purloined stems. Mine glances at my flowers sometimes when he's dictating a letter at my desk and then quickly looks away, as though it offends him to look need in the face. I think of him when I empty the rank water down the kitchen sink, the rotting potato stink of a swamp hiding a dead body. It's strictly against my office philosophy to buy fresh flowers for my own desk. This is also why I don't keep pictures of my loved ones taped to my computer and why I keep the essentials of my life in my backpack at all times. I am prepared to leave town at a moment's notice and never look back.

·   ·   ·

The following arrives in a sealed envelope with a pale turquoise strip and white lettering with CONFIDENTIAL printed in block letters, taped over the flap. I slide my letter opener underneath, break the seal:

PRIVATE AND CONFIDENTIAL MEMORANDUM

TO:	*All Partners*
FROM:	*Managing Partner*
RE:	*Interoffice Bouquets*

The following guidelines are recommended for the purchase of condolence/congratulatory arrangements for office personnel:

Partners	*$80–$125*
Associates	*$75–$95*
Secretaries	*not to exceed $35*
Office Services	*below $35*

The firm maintains an account at Flowers from the Heart, Inc. Whenever possible, please include a client charge.

A temp sits next to me today, an actress. She'll be working all week. Eyeing my bagel she says, "I'm on a special diet. I eat soup." The night before, she tells me, she cooked up a big vat of soup made of a whole cabbage, onions, carrots, parsnips, turnips. I lose track of the vegetables. She holds up a grayish plastic tub, a witch's brew slurping against the sides, and places it reverently in the middle of her desk where it sits all morning. I long to pour it into my After Dark fish tank on my computer screen. During lunch the first day, she recites the complete Soup Diet to me in a sonorous, biblical voice, intoning Day One through Day Seven. It sounds like a poem, each stanza ending, "and then I eat Soup." Her hair is frizzy and she wears a long flowing skirt and a draped top. Telltale sponge marks (for certain, last night's dribbled Soup) appear each morning on her rambling bosom (she's staying in the city for the week on a friend's sofa). We become close, the way you do with one-night stands. Leaning back in our chairs, heads turned sideways, we tell our life stories. Whenever the phone rings, we break off our stories midsentence and answer, taking the opportunity, receivers still at our ears, to also check our home machines. I call my machine far more frequently the week she is here, as though I, too, may suddenly receive a callback from the director of an off-Broadway play. I tell her how to make long-distance calls. She offers me slices of raw fennel and celeriac. She doesn't offer me any of The Soup, which she heats in the microwave several times a day and shamelessly bears back to her desk, leaving a cabbagey wake.

At 11:30, not even lunchtime, she asks if I would mind heating it for her as I'm on my way to the kitchen anyway. I don't bother explaining that the only thing I occasionally microwave at work is my coffee when it gets cold. Even Chinese food that someone else delivered seems too revealing and dangerously malodorous, let alone some odd concoction made at home on a lonely weekend evening, containing all the weird things in your fridge. I'm nervous that while I'm doing Quick-On for two minutes, as she has requested, someone will come in and think that this fart-smelling hippie broth in the middle-aged Tupperware belongs to me. I undernuke it so I'll be out of there before anyone comes in, and watch her slurp around a hunk of cauliflower sitting in the middle of her white plastic spoon, a faded, deep-sea treasure. I wait for Mine to say something, but his nostrils only flare as he stands at my desk. The Smell. I wonder if he will report it to Dragon Lady. Temp is oblivious, raising her eyebrows in a Theater 101 gesture of betrayal. The Soup is cold.

Little Pregnant One temped all night last night and comes into work this morning exhausted. She works a secret third shift at a huge, formal law firm where the temps have to wear suits and pumps, like middle-of-the-night flight attendants. I always know when she's been up all night and will be walking into walls by four o'clock. The telltale signs: her slight, bunionish limp first thing in the morning and the pint of oatmeal she brings from the other law firm's cafeteria sitting jauntily on her desk in a striped cardboard container, a half-inch of maple syrup glazing the surface, simulating a wholesome morning cheeriness. When I look over later she's sagging downward like a dying swan, the wings of her shoulder blades caving inward. I go up behind her quietly so as not to startle her and place each hand firmly on her shoulders. She comes to, blinking.

I often cover for her while she goes into her boss's office to nap on his sofa when he's out at a meeting. When Call Girl buzzes my desk with the warning that her Mine is back and on his way down the hall, I tiptoe in and touch her arm. Once she wouldn't wake up, her mouth was frozen open and she was snoring, one foot dangling over the edge of the sofa, a bright red toenail poking through her stocking. I shook and shook her, first on her forearm, moving up to her shoulder, finally patting her cheek in a delicate slap. Finally she opened her eyes with a little scream and we quickly left his office. As we walked out we were both straightening our clothes as if we'd been having sex. She had sleep creases in her face as she stared up at him, wide-eyed with a look of glazed reverence, about to erupt in post-traumatic stress symptoms, silently thanking him. He knows, but never says anything, a tiny charity.

In celebration of surviving the morning, I eat Japanese food for lunch every Monday. I've discovered a small restaurant with a tatami room where they allow a single person to sit at a table in the corner facing a bamboo and rice paper window. I call ahead of time to make sure I can get this table.

"Table one," the lady who answers the phone always says in a singsong voice.

"Table one," she repeats firmly when I arrive, ushering me into the small room where I slip off my shoes and slide onto the cool, rush mat.

I order only tea and a glass of lemon water instead of sake as it's the beginning of the week and the glow would only make me feel mournful. I always order the special sashimi and an extra uni hand roll. The waitress brings me a hot washcloth with a pair of wooden tongs. When I know it's sashimi day, I start thinking about this hot washcloth in the middle of the morning while I'm typing. Suddenly it will enter my mind and I can't stop thinking about it, as though someone is dipping it down in front of my screen, luring me away. This also happens with the horseradish. I anticipate the rush at the top of my nose, and think about the way it blends in with the soy sauce when you massage it with the tips of the chopsticks in the blue lacquered side dish. These thoughts are sometimes so intense that my taste buds begin to prickle and I salivate. I recognize this as boredom.

I scrape the chopsticks together until they're smooth. I drink the miso soup directly from the bowl. Although I've been coming here for a while, I'm still not sure of the correct way to eat a hand roll, which is cone-shaped and comes in its own dainty trapeze-like swing. A table of businessmen nearby pick up their bowls of soup and drain them noisily. This kind of group activity at lunch makes me feel lonely. No one is picking up my check. I stare at the hand roll, then tweeze it up with my chopsticks and nibble at it, enjoying the salty hairiness of the eel. While the hand roll takes only a few bites to eat, it becomes damp with soy sauce in the process and begins to fall apart. I have become somewhat adept with chopsticks, nevertheless by the end of lunch there is a mess on my wooden board, and too many rice grains in my dipping bowl of soy sauce. I am often ashamed when I've finished a sushi lunch and worry that I smell of fish. I hate that joke about women smelling of fish, but still, I wash my hands carefully afterwards in the miniature bathroom. I'm so sad that it's over for the week I almost cry. It's too expensive to do more than once, and there's also the worry about amoeba lodging permanently in a vital organ. I know I should invite someone from the office to go to this lunch with me, but I always end up going alone.

Near the end of the week, when I'm ready to use chopsticks again, I go to a Chinese restaurant. I do this alone as well.

These are my Chinese lunch fortunes over the past two months:

Prosperity will knock on your door soon.
You may at one time be impractical, sporty or intensely restless.
Your existence has a positive contribution to mankind.
What you left behind is more mellow than wine.
Keep on charging the enemy.

I always break open the fortune cookie with the orange slice still in my mouth. To eat the cookie first ruins the particular sweetness of the orange. I eat one flap of the cookie and read my fortune, then tuck it into a special compartment of my wallet. I keep all my fortunes, having decided that to dispose of them is bad luck. Fortunes are the perfect size and shape to hold a phone number. Once I wrote my number down on the back of a fortune. I'd shared a lunchtime table at Hot Wok because there were no others available. My fortune that day read, *You will meet a handsome dark stranger and he will learn to love you.* I was embarrassed by the simple prescience of this, as though I had read about this trick in a singles dating manual. The man wasn't particularly handsome or dark. He ordered an egg roll, fried dumplings, and lo mein, and we talked. I worried already about his attraction to fat/cholesterol. He never called me. I sometimes wonder if the fortune, when he turned it over and read it, scared him away.

Another time I used the back of a fortune to figure out my cycle while I was at lunch. When I came back to my desk late that afternoon, Mine was standing there staring down at the small slip of paper in his hands, his glasses lifted, puzzling over it. With the tenacious, roaming nature of a milkweed pod, it had attached itself to one of his documents. Pulling it from between his fingers, I said, "Excuse me, but I believe that's my fortune," and tucked it back in my jacket pocket and immediately picked up the phone, standard diversionary tactic. Later, I used the lucky numbers on this compromised fortune to buy a Lotto ticket, playing reverse psychology with fate.

Born Again and I have had synchronized periods for close to a year. She's been asking me all morning when we're expecting them because she's late and she's worried; it ruined her weekend. Am I worried too? If I get mine, that means she'll be getting hers any second. Last month she created a table on the computer to track our cycles. She keeps it on a disk marked Personal and Confidential in a locked holder on her desk. Last time she retrieved it, she tried creating a what-if scenario on the computer involving our periods, using the Optimizer to find the production mix, and ended up losing the whole thing. Now all that valuable menstrual data is permanently unreachable.

EXCERPT FROM FIRM NEWS BULLETIN:

Thanks to a piece in The New York Times *recently, in which 2% milk was compared to the fat content of bacon, membership in the Skim Milk Club has skyrocketed! Due to this popularity, the firm has offered to take over the expense of the skim milk from the club. Beginning next Monday, membership in the Skim Milk Club will be free!*

Once a month, I spend the afternoon paying clients' credit card bills. One client lives on a ranch in Argentina and comes to New York on business so that his wife can go shopping. I run down the bill slowly with my finger, stopping at each entry and reliving their day, imagining what they bought. Shopping in the morning at Bendel's, Saks, Tiffany's, lunch at The Four Seasons. Shopping at Ann Taylor and Bloomingdale's, back to Tiffany's. When did she decide she needed *two* cut crystal bud vases at $425 apiece? Dinner at La Côte Basque. Total for the weekend: twenty-three thousand dollars and thirty-six cents. It's my job to write out the check to American Express. The words are so long they hardly fit into the space. By the time I get to the cents, it's mouse writing. I typed a fax for the client's wife once. Her hair is jet black, pulled back in a bun, and she has the kind of slick moist-looking skin, slightly tanned, that glows with wealth. Her lips are bright red and she wears a black cashmere cape that I secretly stroke when she leaves it draped over Mine's guest chair. I imagine her in their hotel room at the Pierre, clothes strewn across the bed and floor, ordering cups of espresso and bottles of champagne, having evening dresses brought up for viewing. Once I delivered a sealed envelope to her husband at the hotel. I called from down in the lobby and she answered in her high, staccato English. She was alone. I wanted to invite her downstairs for a glass of wine. I imagined her sweeping into the lounge in one of her lacy South American shawls and embracing me. I could actually feel the silky fringe against my arms. I hung up the house phone feeling nauseous with yearning.

I like to imagine her now in a huge airy house, the boxes and packages and clothes spilling over a leather sofa. Horses gallop outside. She always says *mi amor* when she answers the phone now and hears that it's me. For helping his wife, the client bought me designer perfume in a bottle that looks like a human organ.

We are always either too hot or too cold. In the winter, or between the seasons, like now, it's too hot and the shedding begins, first the jacket, then the sweater, down to something short-sleeved, too revealing. Snow might be falling yards away. Summer air conditioning is freezing, blasts of arctic air from the ceiling vent requiring maintenance men and their ladders, sometimes a desperate stopgap measure on our parts, a piece of cardboard from the back of a legal pad stuck inside the vent, unsightly but effective. Wearing a sweater in the middle of August makes you feel crazy, menopausal. We're supposed to be grateful for our indoor weather; for the most part we are. Everyone has a different perception of the temperature. They complain out loud, some warm, some cold, you agree with the next complainer, that temperature, that moment; in all likelihood you felt that way earlier anyway and might feel it again, all in all it's simply easier to agree, to go on complaining with the next one. The only bond formed: anger at the management, the building at large, the shivering or the pulling at the neck, the "phew," the vague sense that underneath our individual thermostats we are joined in exciting rebellion. Vent politics.

They don't like it when we stop and talk, but we can't help it. It's like standing in the front yard and someone stops by the garden fence. One of Them comes down the hall, dictating. Secretary glides away, midstory. We have eyes at the backs and sides of our heads. Even when we're facing our screens and typing a thirty-page document, we see. Dragon Lady keeps track of who's late and who takes more than an hour for lunch. She keeps her own private calendar with dates and times. Her Mine always brings her a precision watch back from Zurich. She brandishes this on her freckly wrist around the corral for a week, an elegant manacle. We think she's paid to spy.

I worry that I have carpal tunnel syndrome. I imagine myself gardening and cooking and using my vibrator wearing a thick wrist brace. I'm always adjusting my chair up and down by the little lever underneath, trying to make sure that my wrists are exactly even with the keyboard and that there's not an unnatural tilt or droop there. Every hour or so, I stop typing and perform circles with my wrists, first one way, then the other. It's already too late to get workmen's comp for this.

I use an anti-glare filter over the computer screen, which

makes the letters slightly fuzzy, so that my eyes strain to make out the words. I experiment with the colors on my screen, making the background Cinnamon Tulips and the border Black Leather. I always end up returning to my blue lagoon. That's the deep dark blue screen that beckons like a swimming pool. It soothes my eyes.

The concept of After Dark screen-savers, the fact that your computer needs to stay busy at all times so it won't burn out by staying still, strikes me as overprotective. Our computer environments are one of the few things we are allowed to decide on ourselves, so we switch often. Choosing your screen-saver is like choosing bedroom wallpaper. You like it at first, and then you get bored, you're ready for a change, and then you're not sure it's what you wanted. Bad Dog is my favorite screen-of-the-month. Each morning I look forward to seeing him as though he's my own puppy, wagging his tail, waiting for food. "Good morning, Bad Boy," I say, half under my breath. I long to follow him inside the jagged holes he tears in my screen, to crouch next to him, help him chew the wires. I wish he really were gnawing on the network, eating documents. He raises his leg and pees on the trash can while Mine stands at my desk. He turns away from my computer screen in disgust as though these acts are real. I wait for his complaint via confidential interoffice e-mail.

I realize I have a problem. I've been walking around the office feeling jealous that other people have Bad Dog on their screens. I go back to my desk and sit in front of my computer, longing to swat his behind with a rolled-up section of the newspaper. I banish Bad Dog to the doghouse and enter calmer, more philosophic realms. For a while I live with Fish Pro, the deep-sea screen. I select bubbles, ocean floor, watch the fish swim lazily by, a cat eyeing the tank. I like the jellyfish's long sexy tentacles, imagine them swishing back and forth across my back, stage one of a car wash, see the jellyfish move obligingly to cover Mine's head in a gooey shower cap, wrap its tentacles around his neck. I put myself down there, deeper and deeper, naked, unprepared, a mermaid suffering the bends. I wonder what screen-savers are designed to save us from. Mine's alternates daily between Geo Bounce and Daredevil Dan.

There's a new screen-saver called Make Sense. Prophetic word salad in crayon colors flashes across the screen.

ELVIS IS NOT A TESTY LASAGNA.

DUNG EXPLODES.

MY DOG BO-BO'S MOTORCYCLE NEEDS TO SLEEP.

THEREFORE I HACKED.

MICK JAGGER RAN.

I try not to leave this screen-saver unattended, worrying about the exposed, pre-straitjacket nature of this nonsense. I leave one of Mine's documents on the screen instead: *Words are never to be rejected as meaningless or repugnant, if by any reasonable construction they may be made consistent and significant.*

COULD OUR BRAINS EAT HIM?

Shoes collect under our desks. I leave my first pair of black, low-heeled pumps at the office because I know I'll never wear them anywhere else. These have become my office shoes, they live here, middle-aged and low-slung. Next to them rests a more hopeful, sexy pair, a relic of the time I had a date right after work. I ended up not wearing them because I worried that they would make me too tall. It was a blind date. Like a bloodhound, I smelled his aftershave the moment I walked into the Sheraton lobby. There he was, a small neat man with a shiny lightbulb-shaped head sitting in one of the red leather armchairs sipping a martini. He had on a wool overcoat with a nap that stuck straight up, the hairs glistening like a small, valuable dog's under the lamp-light. The top of his head was tan and looked oiled. I walked right past him. I went to another Sheraton and had a vodka and tonic at the bar.

A pair of off-white drugstore stockings are hidden in my private bottom desk drawer which smells of the vitamin power packs I keep stashed in a Pendaflex file. I bought these thinking they might give me the energy to leave my job. I keep meaning to throw them away. One morning I downed a power pack right before lunch and within minutes my body began to burn, starting with my thighs and hands and moving in a visible red stain up my body. "Niacin flush," pronounced Dragon Lady as she walked by, hardly stopping. My face was still beating blood and everyone was clustered around my desk wondering if they should call an ambulance, when Mine walked up to my desk holding a tape out in his open palm as if it was an offering.

"Can you just do this one?" he asked.

Some of us keep our shoes in a neat row pushed toward the back wall under our desks. Others have scattered collections, some of the shoes upright, some lying on their sides as though kicked off before sex. This collecting is called relaxing into a job. Although she tries to maneuver politely around them, Cleaning Angel pushes the shoes around at night when she vacuums. I also carry shoes around with me in my bag, prepared for anything. The more shoes I have under my desk, the more I carry around, the fewer I have at home. I have trouble finding a pair to put on my feet on weekends. My snow boots have ended up here, too. Seeing them sitting under there, dusty brown suede with salt marks in a rick-rack pattern, depresses me. They seem too heavy to take home now that spring is almost here and I keep forgetting to bring a bag to carry them in. I'll look like one of the mentally ill on the subway with no regard for seasons. And how do you know when it will snow again? Perhaps for the first snow, I will be at the office and not at home, so the boots are exactly where they should be.

Once I decided to get my shoes shined on my lunch hour. I asked Born Again's Mine how much to tip. He gave me a smirk and then told me, as if he was telling me how to pay for a hooker. I went to the shoe repair place a block from the office. I had the money ready in my pocket. All three men waiting before me wore wingtips with the deep, tough-looking chestnut shine that comes from years of polish buildup. Sitting up on their high wooden chairs, feet planted apart, two were reading newspapers; one was talking on his cellular phone. They seemed perfectly content to be trapped by a stranger holding their feet down with a taut, dirty cloth. I hadn't known how sexy it was to have a forefinger pressed inside a cloth running hard back and forth across your leather toes. My shoes seemed too shiny afterwards and I was embarrassed.

At four o'clock I always take off my office shoes and put my cross-trainers back on. This small rebellion assures me that the remainder of the day will soon be my own. If there is a meeting, I quickly switch my shoes back again. I don't want Peach to see me this way. I feel heavy and lumbering in my white aerobics shoes, a weird office hybrid, part nurse, part duck. I avoid all IOAs after four. It's also around the time Peach's girlfriend starts calling and they make plans. She wears silver rings on every one of her fingers including her thumbs. I've seen them meet in front of the building after work and tongue-kiss.

I put my foot up on the edge of my desk to tie my shoes. I'm not sure if this is rude, like putting your shoes on someone's bed. One of the Rest-of-Us passes by and looks at me with raised eyebrows as though I'm scraping dog shit onto my desk. People talk. Who does and doesn't wash her hands after going to the bathroom. My hands are extremely dry. If I wash them each time, particularly with that cheap pink liquid detergent in the pump, the stiffness of my skin interferes with my typing. So I simply turn the water on and stand there, glancing my fingertips by or near the stream. If I need to put on lipstick, and someone else is there in a stall, I turn the water on and stand there doing what I need to do with my hands nowhere near the water. Being thought of as clean is important.

Not-yet-showing Madonna, Esq., marches right out of the stall and out the door, shaking her hair back like a horse, not even pretending to wash her hands. All the secretaries laugh about this. She's on the partner track and doesn't need to care what we think. If the law firm had a yearbook, her favorite quotation would be, "You're leaving already?" Even though she's now pregnant, she still talks on the phone with her feet up on her desk, her pumps crossed so you can see the soles of her shoes as you walk by her office; she tucks her skirt in around her thighs so you can't see up her skirt. Along with various pictures of babies on her credenza, none of which is hers, is a large framed photograph of a tree starkly outlined against snow. This was taken on a skiing trip, although its real purpose is to demonstrate that despite the fact that she is a successful attorney, she is still a human being who more than anything admires Nature and Art.

They brought in an expert to test the air. They discovered that it contains an unusually high level of hair and dry skin particles. Every office has an air/hair/skin ratio, but we have a higher concentration than most. I happened to see a report left in the Xerox machine. I look up at the wall vents and imagine hair and dry skin raining down on me in a gentle shower. I think about this every time I breathe. I try not to take deep breaths.

Biggest Mine brings us in a treat this afternoon. He marches a full circuit around the corral making his fake Santa Claus ho-ho sounds that he uses all year-round to talk to us. "Help yourself to the goodies in the conference room," he booms. Although the word is already out, we flock in obediently, crowding around the long marble conference room table. It's four o'clock on Monday afternoon and he's brought us the leftover bagels and half-full tubs of chive and raisin and walnut cream cheese from his father's funeral that morning. The bagels are spread out on overlapping paper doilies covering a disposable silver tray sprinkled with sesame and poppy seeds and round grease marks. We all cluster around and stare, as if we are at a supper for the homeless. Born Again, who retains some of her church instincts, picks up a white plastic knife and starts carving a piece from a dry-looking cinnamon raisin bagel. Most of us have secret snack drawers in our desks, and the freebies are hard to completely ignore as there is a scrounge mentality among us. I take a small piece of bagel that Born Again offers to me, balanced on the end of the knife as though it's a slice of birthday cake. We all stand there nibbling like mice. We go back to our desks. We don't bother to thank Biggest Mine next time he circles the corral. As usual, there is an unspoken awareness among us that his pride in his own generosity is all the thanks he needs.

Biggest Mine's secretary always wears scarves, even in the summer. He gives her scarves on all occasions that require a token of his esteem. She, in turn, feels obliged to noose her long, ex-dancer's neck in these small, silky reminders of her servitude. Sometimes she wears a nautical looking square with an anchor/chains/flag motif. She arranges it so that it falls in a stiff triangle pointing exactly down the middle of her back and ties it in a Girl Scout knot in front. Other days she wears flowing pastel chiffon scarves that she wraps around her neck just once like a bandage, allowing the long ends to drape down her back. I imagine her scarves getting caught in the elevator doors on the inside and the elevator descending and her getting instantly strangled, the way Isadora Duncan did when her scarf got caught in the wheel of a car. Many of us dislike Scarf because she has learned how to make a great deal more money than the rest of us. I try to avoid participating in petty office jealousies, although I realize that envisioning her death by strangulation, perhaps even decapitation, is a manifestation of some envy.

Dublin comes by my desk with pictures of her Bermuda vacation already stuck in a miniature album. She sits on the opposite side of the corral, but likes to roam. She's always making long-distance calls to Ireland and charging the firm and then denying that she made them.

At least once a week, someone comes by with pictures. "Here are my vacation pictures," they'll say, never "Would you like to see my vacation pictures?" There are always multiple shots from imperceptibly different angles of the person in a bathing suit, sitting on a beach or by a hotel pool. You're looking at them wearing a small bikini, at their cleavage and exposed thighs and belly, and you say, "The water is such a beautiful color!" You both overlook the fact that they are almost naked, just as when you see a picture of a newborn with a close-up of the baby's genitals, you don't comment on them. There are always pictures of the inside of the hotel room with a reflection of the flash in the round motel-style vanity mirror.

Dublin and her friend have bad sunburns so that the skin tones and the cheap furniture make the photographs look like Polaroids from a low-budget porn movie. She's sitting on the edge of the bed with a strange man in a white suit who has his arm around her bare shoulder. "Oh, you look so sunburned!" I say, noticing the smooth cement expanse of the king-sized bed and imagining the red-and-white-striped bodies thrashing around, sloshing piña coladas.

"We're just about to go down to dinner in that one," she says.

"The hotel looks very nice," I say. I don't ask who the man is.

Mine's wife always gets her hair braided when they go to the islands. Her scalp burns in rows and he takes aerial photographs.

Someone is splattering the toilet seats in the ladies' room. This has become an office scandal. The women talk about it so the men can't hear. It could be any one of us. This afternoon a computer-generated sign decorated with a genie in an oversized turban making a wish over a crystal ball appears taped inside every stall door: *Before you leave, make sure that the toilet is* _flushed_ *and the seat is* _wiped._ (Albertus Extra-Bold, 22 point). We all look at each other speculatively, the secretaries, wondering which one of us it is. Who stands so high and angrily over the seat and sprays up and back against the wall like a dog?

Last summer over the Fourth of July weekend, new toilets were installed, toilets that flush automatically and mysteriously, triggered by some motion of the feet or shifting of the body. The rushing water pulls at you like you're the dark underside of a pier. When you stand up and look, everything is gone, sucked away before you've had a chance to see it, a strange intrusion, like taking a litter box away from a cat. Even attorneys need to look at their feces and mentally paw, *nudum pactum, nolo contendere.*

Thank you for <u>not</u> sharing, the sign says at the bottom.

Little Pregnant One pulls her half-slip down over her belly and strokes the zipperlike mark the elastic makes, only half hiding behind my desk. Friday will be her last day. When she needed to go home for bed rest or she'd lose the baby, her bosses worried out loud that she hadn't been eating right, but secretly worried even more about her job performance. She'd throw up in her wastebasket, bent double under her desk, holding her long black hair bunched at the back of her neck out of the way. Hers said they understood, *but stay just tonight, only till ten, you can take a car home (we can't live without you).*

Every day after lunch, she walks by my desk cupping her hands under her belly, knees slightly bent, as though carrying a bruised watermelon. She borrows my office sweater, which hangs from the back of my chair like a gutted cat. When she returns it to me, the droopy knitted collar smells of prenatal vitamins. She's stockpiling paper towels and bottles of Tropicana, unofficial maternity benefit.

Between three and four o'clock is snack time at the office. This ritual might include a Coke, a small bag of Frito Lay potato chips and a York's Peppermint Pattie one day, an apple and a bottle of Evian the next, the schizophrenic nature of health concerns proving to be an ongoing hazard of office life. Sugar, caffeine, and/or salt are key. A druglike mood enhancer is essential at a time when more dignified cultures are experiencing some version of siesta. Many of the Rest-of-Us are capable of eating entire bags of pretzels or whole boxes of donuts at a sitting, attempting to render this activity less grotesque by leaving the opened bag on top of our desks, the inviting maw turned toward passersby, assuaging guilt. Suddenly disgusted, we tape the bags dramatically closed with layers of Scotch tape, overlapping staples and binder clips, Houdini/eating-disorder safe.

The office candy jar is shaped like a goldfish bowl, a slanted mouth for easy access, a Tupperware-type lid. The jar is almost always full, but its level descends rapidly. Anonymously and publicly by Them, mostly by the Rest-of-Us, the jar is continuously filled with candy, the taking out and the putting back in an ongoing flow of greed and repentance. Late morning, hypoglycemic Mine sidles up guiltily and leaves with a handful of miniature Hershey bars. Others march up and announce their intentions with bravado, or say nothing at all. Everyone has a story, no one cares. Who's cheap, who takes the most, who never contributes, who is greedy, who is fat, who is anorexic. *Oh, I shouldn't, I'm on a diet. Oh my God, no more Snickers left. He's such a pig. She's such a bitch. Milky Ways suck.* Hands reach in and grope; some gobble standing right there, others scurry back to their desks to hide and savor, tigers and squirrels. I favor miniature Reese's cups and the occasional white chocolate Kiss. I reach in and take just one, over and over again, revel in the thick sweet slime of a Hershey's Kiss tucked inside my cheek until the skin there feels like warm wet velvet, about to tear, and my desk becomes littered with tiny silver balls.

Now that all of Them speak into miniature tape machines, full frontal contact with Us is mostly avoided, a mutual blessing. Mine buzzes me on the phone. "Bring your pad in," he says. He likes to do this at exactly one minute to five, just as he hears me shuffling my stuff into my bag, the I'm-going-home zipper sound they can't stand.

The classic Doris Day pose, legs crossed, calf splayed out, is surprisingly functional, the slope of the knee providing a little tilted writing desk on which to place the steno pad (amazing that some paper factory still makes them, spiral at the top, line down the middle, pale, institutional green). The foot of the crossing leg, pump dangling, is now free to swing close to the polished front of the mahogany desk, a reflex test gone haywire.

He sighs and leans back in his swivel chair showing me two damp three-quarter moons under his arms. His suit jacket is as usual hanging over the back of the other chair, folded inside out so that the monogrammed silk lining and Armani label show. "Pursuant to our conversation of even date," he begins. I once asked him what "even date" meant. He peered at me sternly over the tops of his glasses, lifted his eyebrows and didn't answer.

He shifts in his chair and looks out the window, picks his nose a little, disguises this action with a vigorous brushing of the tip with his forefinger. My pen stays poised half an inch from the paper, my eyes cast down, I write the word "Fuck" and then join the top and the bottom of the *F* with the *u* and the *c* with a couple of curved lines and then add two nipple dots in the circles I've made and turn the whole into a Miracle bra, then crosshatch vigorously over it.

This is my method for faking fast longhand. I write as quickly as I can, trying to make the substantive words legible, not worrying too much about the connecting stuff. When he's finished dictating I go straight to my computer without talking to anyone and spill back everything I can remember, generally not a hundred percent. He never really notices the difference, proving my legalese gobbledygook theory. He refused only once to sign a letter and marked it up with red pen in outraged schoolteacher circles and flung it on my desk.

A few of the old-timers here can't deal with going on the network. They pick up their mouses from the little rubber pads next to their computers and dangle them in the air by their cords as if they're tails. "We don't do Windows," they say loudly in chorus. When they're in their bosses' offices they sit slumped over their steno pads looking resigned. They're like those old racehorses they put out to pasture to eat grass.

Mine stands behind my chair just to my left. The southwest corral has cleared out and we're suddenly alone together. Out of the corner of my eye, I can see the burnished wing tips, the way the cuffs of his pants perfectly cut the arch of his shoes. He has a nervous habit of rocking, a habit to which he is oblivious. The fabric of his trousers trembles slightly with the movement. One knee straightens and then the other, then bends, straightens again, a puppet's dance. I imagine this habit beginning when he was a teenager, looking at a girl's breasts, staring into and beyond her sweater, wondering how it would feel to stroke them with his finger, to touch, to squeeze. Making six figures many times over, still he indulges in adolescent clumsiness. Standing behind me, he begins to scratch his crotch. It starts with a small movement, an animal scrabbling, hardly discernible at first. He adjusts himself in his underwear, one knee bending sideways, a small, irritable plié, the Mine Special. Two sentences later, he's scratching again.

*   *   *

ATTORNEY CHARGES:

Drafted condolence note to client's widow. (We join you in mourning your tragic loss . . .) Faxed same. 50 minutes. Charge to client. $275.00.

I've begun treating the night Cleaning Angel like a mother I never see. I rearrange the junk under my desk, spreading it around, pushing things into corners with my toes, stuffing other things into drawers. I regard this underworld as though it is invisible, my private room. I leave brimming coffee cups in the wastebasket the way I used to leave them lined under my bed as a teenager. I imagine what happens when she lifts the wastebasket and tips it upside down into her canvas dumpster, liquid splashing, the way she will shake her head in disgust. I pray she forgives me as she would a daughter. I vow daily to clean up my act, to organize under my desk, to empty out cups before throwing them away, to not waste so much soda, to disperse the wedding confetti that sifts gaily onto the rug from my 3-hole punch, to write her a note of apology. Coming in to my desk in the morning, to the shiny new plastic bag lining my wastebasket, the way everything is so neatly vacuumed, is like returning to a motel room after maid service and finding your underwear still there, but draped differently. My mess grows and spreads under the desk like a sweet moss. Each day, I leave my wastebasket overflowing with cans and cups under my desk, Saturday afternoon at the beach.

Monday's miracle: That it's Monday night. (This countdown is called a life.)

TUESDAY

THE WEEK BEFORE SECRETARY'S DAY, MINE SAT IN HIS OFFICE, tipped back in his chair, reading a pamphlet from Katharine Gibbs Secretarial School, his head dipped at a considering angle:

> *Give the gift of our Recharger Workshop for Secretaries Day. . . . Gibbs one-day power workshops are designed to raise Performance Level, Productivity, and Morale. Help your Secretary to successfully manage conflicts for win-win solutions! Help your Secretary to be perceived as the best! Help her learn to produce the correspondence every executive in your company will envy!**
> **Tuition is tax deductible.*

I lined up a spot on Mine's head, just behind his ear, in the crosshairs.

Say it with . . .

Not getting flowers on Secretary's Day is on a par with not getting valentines from your classmates back in fourth grade. Not only is Mine not taking me to lunch today, but the whole office looks like a funeral parlor, except for my desk. He passes by with averted eyes and bustles out. He has a lunch date with a big client. By now I know that everyone is feeling sorry for me and glad that they're in safe possession of their pink sweetheart roses with baby's breath or multicolored long-stemmed imported tulips in a distressed wicker basket.

We all stroll through the garden show, the Rest-of-Us, the Mines and the Almost Mines, pretending we're not taking a mental tally: who got the blue ribbon, who got the short-stem prize. The categories of caring are complex. Receiving flowers in the morning means your Mine thought about it last night or on the way to work. Midmorning signals a guilty nudge at the sight of early-morning bouquets, enough for Them to run out to the corner Korean market and grab a bunch of 24-hour dying stowaways from down south. Late afternoon and nothing to show means either the delivery of the extra large Stargazer lilies got held up, dramatic late appearance to *oohs* and *aaahs,* or you're screwed. The dried rosebud topiary from one of the Almost Thems that won me so much attention last year is at home near my stove, covered in oily cobwebs. I'm dreaming of magnificent snapdragons.

Last year Mine took me out to lunch for Secretary's Day. He ordered a quart of Pellegrino water without asking me what I wanted. Large, bristling dark green salads simply arrived.

"Are you satisfied with your attitude?" he asked, his kind of small talk, dabbing his lips with his napkin and then pulling away and looking at it as though expecting to find lipstick there.

"I'm not sure what you mean by that," I said, folding, refolding, and finally stabbing a large red lettuce leaf with my fork and skating it toward the gutter of the plate. Odd to be eating from such large plates at lunch, with bits of parsley stuck to the rims as though they hadn't been washed, although I knew this was simply artful presentation.

"Un otro," he said in his Long Island Italian. Another bottle of Pellegrino arrived with a flourish. I knew the waiter was smirking. I was reassured that it was not at me, an event like Secretary's Day fostering all-round goodwill among subservients.

"Self-analysis can be a valuable tool," he said. "What I mean to say"—he paused—"are you satisfied with your performance outlook?"

After he delivered the pasta, the waiter hovered over the table with a bowl of Parmesan cheese and sprinkled both of our plates with a snowy drift. I twirled a bite of pasta until it had formed a safe, pale spindle. The cheese was so sharp it took little bites out of my tongue and the roof of my mouth. Mine ate his pasta by twirling his fork vigorously inside a large spoon. Flecks of sauce flew out and sprinkled his plate as if from a fertilizer machine, but he didn't seem to notice. Did he ever think about having sex with me? I imagined him in his pajamas, paring his toenails into a wastebasket.

"I think what you're asking is . . ." I began slowly, stalling. A vein pulsed on the right side of his head near his eye. We both looked up and saw another Mine and his secretary at a nearby table getting ready to leave. We nodded and waved and turned back to our plates. I didn't finish my sentence. It had no end anyway. Mine looked relieved as they stopped by our table, and together with the other Mine stood there looking through his wallet for his credit card. His secretary and I rolled our eyes at each other. From her safe vantage point behind her Mine's back, she yawned, patting her mouth with her red-polished fingertips, mimicked ditching her foil swan-with-a-handle doggie bag behind her shoulder, and made an abrupt off-the-cliff shoving motion at the back of his raincoat.

•   •   •

My first Secretary's Day with Mine, I took my tulips home on the subway, the vase stuck upright between my knees in a shopping bag. My hands dipped into the bag and I started pulling off the petals and nesting them together in my palm. People kept looking over. What was she doing? Clearly, I wasn't homeless, I wasn't loading a gun. By the time I reached my stop, only the spiky powdery black and yellow insides, stamens, pistils, whatever, were left. Dropping the petals in the bathtub, I filled it with very hot water, intending to bathe along with my underpants and stockings, a time-saver in a busy secretary's day, although the clothes floating at my sides will nudge me sometimes, as though I'm in the company of drowning victims. After draining the bath, I squeezed the tulip petals out and gently laid them on a towel on the floor to dry. The next morning they had the silky soft texture of dried skin. Pulverizing them in my blender, I then placed the petal puree in a little blue bowl on my altar. I stood there cradling my before-work half-cup of coffee at my neck, staring down at them.

Daily I refill the glass of water that stands in the corner of my apartment near the front door to clear my life of evil influences. I repeat certain words that he says in my ear. *"Willful malfeasance,"* I whisper as I lock myself into my apartment at night.

Red roses were delivered to me at the office only once. Everyone assumed they were from a lover, did the usual roses reaction formation: double-take, backtrack, teasing eye contact, stop and bend down, take a long sniff, first one rose then another (since roses no longer smell, this archaic gesture may soon be left out of this performance piece), a brief subtle search for an accompanying card, then everyone just standing there, expecting information. Office roses are everyone's business, a collective romantic entitlement. My red roses, awkwardly numbering a dozen and a half stems, were from Perugina who was fired the month before and was thanking me for having warned her, saving her dignity. I think she had a crush on me, signaled by the extra half-dozen, and the fact that they were red, not pink or yellow. Subway roses, a deep suspicious dried-blood color, they suffered spinal injury in the night and the next morning were broken-necked cartoon characters in need of extra aspirin. I threw them out.

A bunch of the Rest-of-Us are standing at the floor-to-ceiling windows of Mine's office while he's safely at his lunch meeting, looking down. We're on the thirty-seventh floor. Attorneys have views. We prize our miniviews from inside the corral; mine, for example, a half-inch wide strip of salami-red sunset if I lean sideways at just the right time. Making a frame with both my hands cuts out everything except the two rustic-looking water towers on the top of a building below. If I squint, the sea of taxis in the background could be a deep summer field of sunflowers.

"What's it like outside?" someone calls from behind me. People in offices are always asking what the weather is like outside, as if you have information they don't have.

"I don't know," I say, "I haven't been out."

"Is it raining?"

"I can't tell," I say. Amazing that you can only tell when the rain is driving against the windows and the sky turns dark and then everyone gets up and gathers around the windows in Mine's office when he's at lunch and watches as it gets darker, office eclipse, and we all lean into the windows folding our arms as if we're witnessing a miracle, until we finally disperse and go back to our abandoned desks where our cursors are blinking.

"I wish I knew whether to take an umbrella with me to lunch," someone says.

I decide to treat myself to a manicure for Secretary's Day.

The smiling Korean man is there as always, thrusting a paper flyer at me, a different neon color each day, offering the latest manicure/pedicure combination and silk tips special at nearby Sunny Nails.

"Nairls! Nairls!" he screams as I walk by. Some days I brush his hand away from my path, an annoying insect. Today, I take a flyer and smile at him as though he's offered me a personal gift. On these days I remind myself that with his baggy beige sweater and broken teeth he is probably the unemployed father of one of the manicurists. I imagine him shoveling rice into his mouth at the end of the day, going to sleep and dreaming of colored flyers and women with vermilion nails swooping down and scratching out his eyes.

A miniature woman in a smock and a white surgical mask clucks sharply over the dryness of my hands and the tiny ridges in my nails clearly visible under the ultraviolet light. She persuades me to get a deep cream hand oil treatment for just $10.99. Helpless before the thought of being touched during the workday, I nod. She scoops warm cream from a moon-shaped dish plugged into the wall and begins rubbing it into my hands. I close my eyes. She massages deeply into my palms, concentrating on the base of my thumbs and then interlocks our fingers, pushing all ten of hers down onto mine, strong and urgent as a lover. She shakes both my hands and wrists free in an undulating motion as though shaking out a rug, once, twice, in some magical stress-releasing movement of the East. I want to cry, but she has my hands trapped and I can't reach up to shield my eyes. I feel embarrassed in front of the other women who sit, looking bored, their fingertips drooping into glass bowls of suds. I smell organ meats bubbling on the hot plate in the back room. I want to stay and eat from the pot with them. The woman across from me stares raptly at the display of tiny diamonds glued into separate constellations on each nail. Tilting my face up at the ceiling-light grid, I blink tears back, unwilling to face the manicurist's curiously tender eyes above her mask.

Since Mine didn't offer, I decide to take myself out. This two-hour lunch could be the beginning of the end.

I stumbled on McFeeley's one day when I was walking down Ninth Avenue, taking a pair of shoes to get lifts. The cool, old-beer basement smell grabbed me from the sidewalk, the smell of an old man's jacket, inexplicably appealing. There's a permanent bar stool waiting for me next to him on the way down and out.

I walked in the first time because there were no windows, just that smell beckoning me as I passed under an awning. I backtracked, looked to the right and left for a Mine who might be wandering out of leash range, and stepped inside. A row of men and two women sat alone at the bar gazing up glassy-eyed at a hanging OTB screen. They turned around and looked at me, then turned back and buried their noses in their huge, smooth-walled pint glasses. Immediately, I felt at home. The bartender nodded at me imperceptibly; I nodded back, a secret beer drinker's signal.

Way in the back, up a few steps, dark green walls, an Old West saloon look, a bunch of empty tables, a few booths. It only needs a barmaid with deep cleavage and a black velvet ribbon around her neck. Right now, I'm the only customer. I slide into a round booth, over the taped vinyl seat to the back of the curve, and spread both of my arms wide across it. The waiter who shambles over after a good five minutes has a belly that pours like well-kneaded dough over the waist of his black, encrusted pants. His spiral notebook slants down at a weary angle and he stares at me, cross-eyed and sweet, permanently hung over. I order a hot pastrami sandwich on rye and a pint of Bass Ale. While I wait, I start reading yesterday's *Post,* which someone has left bedraggled on the seat, Page Six gossip and sports. I like looking at close-ups of basketball players' arms and legs. I read all the stories from beginning to end: tennis, golf, basketball, baseball, become teary over the one about a young city kid from the projects who wants to be a boxer. The black granulate crust on my hot pastrami is exquisitely, painfully salty. The beer makes me light-headed and flush with a sense of fullness for the world; I could fuck the waiter in the booth right now. I feel lucky and optimistic, something will happen to me soon, maybe I'll never go back to work.

A cheer billows back from the bar. Someone's horse has won. My twinge of sexual generosity past, I fight the urge to sink sideways into my booth, to lie down and stroke the curved green vinyl. I know as though I have been born there, the soothing way it will accept the shape of my body; how I can fold my jacket as a pillow and set it down, how everyone at the bar will ignore me, not meanly, but with a shrug. They will wake me before the five-thirty after-office rush when they need the table. I'll have another pint of beer and some mozzarella fingers.

I pay the check and leave a big tip and walk back to the office wearing my sunglasses, although there's complete, oppressive cloud cover. I eat a whole package of Clorets on the way, pouring them straight from the box, piling one on top of another, smooth and cool and clattering like fake teeth in my mouth. On the elevator going up, I think about how green my tongue and spit must be. I'm by myself, so I put my hand up the front of my dress and inside my underwear, just for a minute, wondering if the security guards at the downstairs desk notice on their shadowy gray screens. I'm a little drunk.

Secretary's Day afternoon. The office kitchen runs out of vases and we become rakishly creative. Snapple bottles, coffee mugs, the fake gold ice bucket. The need to display borders on panic. Mostly the equation is how cheap or generous, how kind, how mean, how ready to kick the dog then turn and give it a bone, shake its muzzle fondly. After lunch, chocolate-covered pretzels and a tiny teddy bear are left on all our chairs by the office tooth fairy. The bear has chemically crusted fur that molts off on my fingers. Where to put this humiliating mascot? Perched on the pencil caddy? On top of my terminal? Cement shoes and into the Hudson? The pretzels come in a fancy tin wrapped in a big purple bow (close-out sale, end of a product line, we decide), congratulations by e-mail late in the afternoon.

I overhear sobbing in a stall. Dublin comes out wiping her eyes under her glasses with paper towels. The skin around them has lightning streaks of red. She's the only one in the northwest corral who didn't get anything. "Nothing," she repeats disbelievingly, running her glasses back and forth under the faucet. She knows it's the most ridiculous of all national observances, but what is more mortifying? "It's the principle, not the fucking roses," she says in a stage whisper through clenched teeth, bending to check for feet. "It's worse than waiting for a corsage on prom night, and I never even went," she says, louder. All she needed was some daisies in a jar.

"You wait, I'll forget where the hold button is on their calls tomorrow."

"I didn't get anything either," I say. "Call Dublin for an hour, firm charge."

. . .

My latest IOA is Plant Man. He's tall and skinny and wears a forest green uniform, shorts and a short-sleeved shirt, and carries around a green plastic watering bucket. He hoists his watering can high over the plants on the desk ledges, plants that are so green they look extraterrestrial under the fluorescents. He sprinkles carefully, dabbing away any drops with his white cloth, attentive as a dental hygienist. I imagine the whispery, horticultural care with which he would make love. His fingers are long and brown and wrinkled from so much water, with sweet leathery knuckles like small faces. He plucks yellow leaves with a single snapping movement and tucks them into a small car-trash caddy buckled at his waist. Without his glasses his eyes are dark brown, and his gaze blurs beautifully. His eyes meet mine over the tops of certain plants. We've laughed together at Mine's bonsai, a present from a client. Never saying a word, we stand and look down at the miniature stone path leading to an eentsy green bench sagging on its gravel under a bit of spindly jade. Secretly, I think we're starving it to death. We stand there for a minute and then he turns on his heel and strides over to drown the ficus next to the window. Stooping, we both reach to collect the same pile of crackling leaves at its base, our knees almost touching for a split second on the rug, his brown bare ones near my tightly pulled stockings and skirt, our hands colliding. I sense Mine's arrival, he's standing in the doorway behind us, watching. I wanted to ask Plant Man a question about my failing tuberous begonia at home, about light and water, now it's too late.

Before I leave my desk at the end of the day, I wipe it down with leftover seltzer or tea as though I work in a Chinese restaurant. I have trouble keeping my desk neat. I worry about being discovered. What if someone were to look closely into my drawers and see the mess? While I am an extremely fast typist and have a modulated, even sensual, speaking voice and pleasant manner, if a secretary's purpose is to organize her boss's life, then I admit to being barely a few steps ahead.

Paper clips mate in the night forming a wild bracelet that will not be contained by my desk caddy. Post-Its disappear the way socks do. Attorneys drop by, scribble a note to Mine and leave with my good black felt-tips. I don't say anything, simply order more from Peach. I hoard yellow legal pads at home. I have learned how to smuggle them out in my bag, ten sleekly vacuum-packed pads at a time. I haven't counted how many of these pads I have, but they now form a yellow wall underneath the desk in my bedroom. Once a week, I vacuum my bedroom, using a special round nozzle brush on this paper stack. I take this opportunity to make sure that all the bindings are perfectly lined up, and the pads not visible from my living room, although this is really an unnecessary precaution. No one in the office has ever come to my apartment, even though my address is available to anyone who cares to learn it in its alphabetical slot on the Personnel Address List, updated every four months. Although this liberty taken by Human Resources offends my sense of privacy, I admit to having taken advantage of this same liberty myself, jotting down a few key addresses and phone numbers in my Casio address computer notebook. Peach's, of course, is there. Coincidentally, he lives only ten blocks from me. And Mine's number, of course.

I once saw a man jump from the building across from the office. Born Again and I were sitting in the conference room after hours with our feet up on the table. Everyone else had already left.

I saw something in my peripheral vision, a blur as though I had blinked and a shadow had passed over my left eye and that was that, not even enough to interrupt our conversation. We heard the sirens wail to silence somewhere right below us and went to the window, still holding our coffee cups, and looked down, our faces pressed sideways against the glass to see the body lying on the sidewalk below and policemen drawing a chalk outline around it and someone else unzipping a body bag. I realized what the blur had been. We were sure we saw an umbrella lying nearby. He was wearing a dark suit. We watched for a while but everything took a very long time so eventually we sat back down and finished our coffee.

What have I done with these office phone numbers? I must admit that occasionally I've called them, although now, with the widespread availability of Caller ID, I am much more cautious about this spying activity. Attorneys, with their suspicious minds and delusional egos, are perfect candidates for such a feature. Twice I've called Mine's home while he was right here in the office. Once I got the answering machine. His wife speaks in a high, slightly breathless voice. "Please don't hang up. Leave us a message and we'll call you back." As far as I can tell she doesn't do much but shop and pick up the kids from school when Milagros, the au pair, isn't around. Once when she answered the phone, I kept her on for a long time, just by audibly breathing. I was staring at the back of Mine's head while I was doing this, and could tell by the angle of his arm that he was picking his nose very quietly, tilting his head down onto his finger so as to use the leverage. His wife was saying into my ear with ever increasing sharpness, "Who is this? Who *is* this? *Who* is *this*? *Who is this?*"

"Your husband picks his nose," I longed to whisper, with an obscene caller's urgency. Immediately after I'd hung up, she called back and asked to speak to Mine. He was on the other line and I had to put her on hold for almost four minutes, timed by the digital clock on my phone base. *Clients first.* The motto her husband lives and breathes.

Mine's daughter has been diagnosed with Attention-Deficit/Hyperactivity Disorder. The disorder takes the brakes off your brain and derails concentration. She takes 20 mgs. of Ritalin every day so she can focus. Mine says the drug has improved her study habits; her grades are now good enough to get her into private school. He doesn't tell me all this directly. I read the doctor's report and hear him discussing it with his wife on the phone.

I pretend I don't see the word *Confidential* typed at the bottom of the envelope, open it anyway, slip the letter knife in and slit the envelope in one smooth motion. After I read the letter, I fold it along the original creases and put it back in the envelope so that if he asks me I can tell him I made a genuine mistake. I'm careful not to get any lipstick on the letter. The person who diagnosed this is a psychiatrist named Dr. Hildemar Ortiz-Schumacher. I think the whole family is being treated by her. When I process the insurance claim, there are a great number of hours billed. The kid has ADHD and the wife has SAD. She uses a Bio-Brite Light Visor, a recent invention that combats Seasonal Affective Disorder, darkness-related depression in the winter. I processed the claim for this gadget and the rejection letter from the insurance company. In the morning sitting at the breakfast table and at night before she goes to sleep, she wears a battery-powered visor that blazes light down on her face, improving her mood. She also has a dawn simulator, a lamp timed to brighten slowly like the rising sun and a portable briefcase-sized light box that she carries into work. All of these items arrived at Mine's office by Federal Express and it was my responsibility to unpack them from their protective styrofoam peanuts. She gets completely hyper and stays up all night working if she wears her visor too much. I heard Mine talking about it to another Mine whose wife has the same problem. This is one of those private conversations that isn't private at all. I'm sitting at my desk pretending I'm not listening, and he's acting as though I'm invisible. My hearing becomes extremely acute, also my memory for detail, the way a wolf's sense of smell must be. I don't turn and snarl at Mine and leap for his throat, simply sit there, blushing all over my body so that my face and my breasts prickle, another ancient involuntary reaction. "It's better than Prozac, less expensive and leaves the libido intact," he says. I think of them making love by the light of her miner's halo, the way all their hairs must stand out.

Sometimes when I talk on the phone, particularly during a long private conversation in which my mouth is pressed to the mouthpiece, or when I am put endlessly on hold by an airline, lipstick becomes embedded in the small holes of the receiver and remains there. When I remember to, I spray the phone with Lysol, although not directly into the receiver, and wipe it with a napkin or two from the collection in my second drawer. Mine and the others are always standing at my desk and grabbing my phone without asking, and certainly would never think to cover the mouthpiece with a hand or a Kleenex. I try not to worry too much about germs. Having enough paper products around is a comfort. I have napkins in all sizes and qualities along with silver paper to-go pots of strawberry jam and raspberry jelly and foil packets of ketchup and mustard, and paper containers of salt and pepper, all of which I take from restaurants whenever possible. I enjoy using the thick, snowy paper napkins from expensive coffee bars for office cleaning chores.

Despite myself, I worry about the amount of paper I waste. Everyone here tells killing trees jokes. Sometimes when I type a letter for Mine I make so many mistakes that I waste sheet after sheet of heavy bond letterhead. Either I've placed the date too high, or the address runs into the printed list of attorney names or, as is most often the case, I make typos. Computers are supposed to make life easier, but spell check tricks me, bounding over certain words and pouncing on others with misleading certainty. It can't be trusted. I have a method for folding these discarded pages so that they become quite small, taking on a triangular yet swanlike shape, a kind of office origami. I have sometimes used upwards of ten sheets for one two-line letter in order to achieve the perfection that Mine requires. It's a well-known fact that certain of Them have the habit of going through wastebaskets after hours. They think we don't know this. I imagine Mine sitting at night with the wastebasket cradled between his knees, pulling out balled-up pieces of paper, smoothing them on his thigh and studying closely the creases and hieroglyphics of my shame. I deny him this satis-faction. Usually, I dispose of the evidence by smuggling the pages out of the office in my bag and throwing them out in a public receptacle at least five blocks away. Even this far afield, I bury my swans.

Every two days I go through a bag of sunflower seeds. I eat them in the afternoon for the salt, and for the distraction. Holding a seed between my front teeth lengthwise, I bite and suck on it until the salt leeches out. By this time the seed is soft enough to break open, and I split the shell lengthwise with my teeth, coax out the tiny sliver of sunflower meat with my tongue. Although I have become quite skilled at this, if I attempt to do it without the help of my fingers, I swallow a good amount of shell. I chew on the remaining shell splinters and then spit the wad of wet fibers out into the little cup made by my fingertips. Sometimes I become so absorbed in doing this that I forget where I am, suddenly aware that I am making loud sucking noises.

It's so easy to get caught at the office doing something mindless and humiliating. You're sitting there bored out of your mind waiting for the sticky minutes to tick by and you can't really do anything substantial and character-building. The classic cartoon comes to life when you get caught doing your nails. Secretary in a tight black skirt with crossed legs and high heels, sitting there chewing gum and filing her nails. It's one of those rhythmic, accessible activities that doesn't cost anything. You sit there sawing, then painting one coat, two coats, hardener, finisher, layer after layer, fanning away the acetone smell, huffing and puffing them dry, typing splay-fingered.

Sometimes we read on Their time. The reason so many of us tend to read crummy, three-inch thick potboilers with hysterically thumbed corners is not that we're stupid, but that we never know when we're going to be interrupted, forced to pretend that we weren't really reading anyway. You put the book down in your lap half under your desk and keep your forehead cupped in your hand as though you have a headache or are a little sleepy, ready to be alert and upright at a split second's notice, a surgeon on call. You pick up a subtle, restless cue that a high-up Mine is making his way down the hall. News spreads from one desk to another, just as when you're driving along the highway and people flash you with their lights, warning of a lurking traffic cop. Even before this, some instinct makes you dog-ear the page or peel off a Post-It without looking down at what you're doing and slide it in at the sex scene and push the book out of the way and turn to your computer or pick up your phone all in one easy motion, like ballroom dancing. Why would anyone read Jane Austen?

A few people are going out after work tonight. I join them with a sinking feeling. After a few vodka gimlets, Dublin starts hugging everyone on her way back from the ladies' room, rocking them in amazingly strong bony arms and getting lipstick on their cheeks. She begins talking about God and Church and the IRA and who in the office she thinks has the biggest dick. Everyone always ends up talking about sex and laughing and I feel sorry for the waiters. Our real lives remain curiously off-limits. We order only appetizers, everything breaded and fried and greasy, buffalo chicken wings and Chinese hot wings and mozzarella fingers and zucchini sticks and potato balls. I don't know if this is really what we want, but this is what we order. No one from Accounting is here, so it takes half an hour to figure out the bill and we all end up paying a fortune, mostly because of the drinks that people who don't like to drink order, expensive ones with cream and three liqueurs. Boyfriends and husbands join us at 9:30. There's the husband of the woman who always hand-washes his shirts, and the boyfriend who is chronically unemployed. They shuffle at the front of the restaurant looking embarrassed.

Will you be all right? ask the ones who belong to someone else, the ones with rides, of us solo after-hours straphangers as we head out into the darkness toward the subway.

"Of course," we answer in chorus, heading off in different

directions to our respective outer boroughs, Dublin weaving a little.

<u>*WITNESSETH*</u>*:*

WHEREAS, the parties hereto are a little drunk.

NOW, THEREFORE, in consideration of the mutual covenants and conditions contained herein, this party herewith pronounces this day officially terminated in the manner specified herein.

WEDNESDAY

WHO INVENTED *HUMP DAY,* THIS SAD, FRUSTRATED CAMEL concept? Not one of Them, surely, they never want to go home. If you're depressed in the afternoon because the week seems endless, ask Fax Guy, he'll do his routine. He'll stand there flirting with you, explaining away the week: *Relax, baby, this is the deal. Just a few more hours to get through and then tomorrow we're on the down-stroke, then it's the day before Friday, and then it's the Weeekennnd! We'll take it twenty-four hours at a time.* No one ever mentions how quickly that goes by and then it's Monday again and your whole life is getting swallowed up, except for those itchy, agonizingly slow minutes in the afternoon, when you feel like you're waiting for a lover who never arrives. You walk around because you're falling asleep, nodding down in your unintended junkie, keyboard player nod, rescuing yourself before discovery. You wish you still smoked so you could go downstairs and hang around outside. You end up having a diet Coke and studying yourself in the bathroom mirror, noting how you've aged. There are never any ice cubes in the afternoon. The soda's warmish, like ones you drink when you're sick.

•   •   •

Mine usually conducts the tour when a new Almost Mine is hired. This morning he brings a New One around to meet everyone, coffee in hand. We are scrupulously excluded from these greeting tours. Filled with good intentions and puppy dog politeness, the newcomer wants to be liked by all; to communicate is human, even among Them. Abandoned in front of one of our desks, the New One must wait until one of Them is off the phone, available to exchange pleasantries. His gaze slides below to where we sit typing, nonspecific goodwill smile plastered there. We look back with a noncommittal glance, not quite smiling, neutral, in the protective way of every oppressed meeting with the Other. Born Again's Mine cuts off his phone call and comes to the office door, hand outstretched. With an uneasy backward look at us, the New One disappears inside. We follow his back with rolling eyes, raised brows, stifled sniggering, junior-high-school-ignored stuff. Wet behind the ears, safely married, plain expensive suits, sensible shoes, degrees on their sleeves, the Almost Mines also don't care that we are overlooked. We may never speak as years go by. "Hello," I say to the New One when he reappears. His gaze slides uneasily over me and then stops, returning, guiltily. He nods at me. "Hello," timidly (*Is it okay? Who is she?*). Mine ushers him away and he follows, never looking back, the pillar of salt thing.

On this legal plantation, a series of embedded codes govern all social interactions. The good morning interaction (a Level C) occurs only if one of Them walks by our desks and there is no one more important in the vicinity. Occasionally, one of Them will initiate a conversation with one of the Rest-of-Us, generally a comment about the weather over the weekend just past (Level B). The

most likely place for this Level B to occur is on the elevator, but
only if no one else is riding in it, the presence of a stranger from
another floor being sufficient to prompt a return to the *Wall Street
Journal.* The Level A interaction is rare, occurring only during
compromising social situations. At the annual Christmas party last
year, for example, Mine stood before me holding his glass of
chardonnay in front of him like a totem. I could see the panic in
his eyes as he brought his glass close to mine and very gingerly
touched its curved side. "Holiday cheers," he said, and jerked his
glass away so quickly the wine sloshed onto my hand.

All week long, Madonna, Esq., has been lumbering around the
office in a medieval maternity smock showing off her first
trimester ultrasound. Somehow this midlife event has melted her
judgment. We've never said more than two words to each other,
although I've heard her throwing up in the ladies' room. Marching
out of the stall, looking pale, she washes her hands vigorously
without meeting my eyes in the mirror. Then she goes right back
into the stall and throws up again and comes out and washes just
the very tips of her fingers, her eyebrows arched up high.

Last weekend, another one of Them gave birth. She worked
until eight o'clock on Friday, had the baby on Saturday afternoon
and was pestering her secretary on Monday morning to find out
what was going on. I'm sure that Madonna, Esq., is getting something in writing from her unborn child to honor this agreement;
this is a technique the Almost Mines must learn in law school, how
to push them out on unbillable time.

Today, for some reason, Madonna, Esq., feels compelled to
share the map of her uterus with me. Accepting this boundary-
smashing artifact from her over the high edge of my desk, I stare
at the miniature human storm, the swirling eye of a hurricane.

"It's a boy," she says.

"Congratulations," I say.

When the egalitarian need–hormones recede, will she ever bring the baby around?

By midweek the following responses appear on the signs in the ladies' room:

Stall no. 1, printed (black pen) inside balloon coming out of genie's mouth: *This warning also goes for whoever's leaving the toilet paper runway on the seat.*

Stall no. 3 (blue felt-tip): *Bronx Zoo? Monkey cage?*

Why is there an electrical outlet under the sink in the ladies' room? It seems a strange place for an outlet, perhaps it was put there by mistake. A large blue oscillating fan, the kind that should be placed in a window in summer, is plugged into the outlet. Occasionally someone turns it on. This doesn't happen only in summer, as the seasons are sealed inside the building. The windows won't open. Like the rest of the office, the bathroom was designed without practical thought. Water pools around the sinks and gathers at the edges so that when we lean into the mirror, a one-inch band of wet stains our clothing above our thighs. Sometimes I go out after work branded this way.

I have been thinking about the outlet. How could we abuse it? Toilet seat naps by a sweet glowing night-light? A blender full of afternoon margaritas, whirring under cover of two taps running? Electric hair curling wand, a full basin of water, inadvertent electrocutions (*incidental damages?*).

A few times a year they ask us to buy stuff from their children. This is, of course, not listed as mandatory in the office personnel manual. At Christmas it's a catalogue offering rolls of wrapping

paper and bows, tins of salted pecans and mixed dried fruit, chocolate thin mints and peanut brittle. One of Them sends around an
e-mail first, warning us: *Brittany needs help on her sixth-grade
Christmas drive. She's determined to come in first! Any assistance in
helping her reach her goal would be greatly appreciated! Happy
Holidays!* The catalogue arrives by interoffice mail. I flip through
it, deciding that this time I will not be pulled in. I've never spoken
to this she-Mine, never laid eyes on her mini-wheeler-dealer
daughter. I flip through the catalogue feeling removed and
unpressured until I reach the ordering page. The names of
everyone in the firm have already been neatly printed out alpha-
betically in the name column. The square boxes next to the names
directly above and below my name are already a forest of X's. My
empty boxes look like a neatly weeded railroad track. In the total
column are sums like $21 and $18. Eighteen dollars' worth of
peanut brittle and salted nuts so that Brittany can experience the
gratification of naked ambition rewarded. I put an X down by a
pound of what sound like glorified raisinets. They come in a "festive holiday tin" that "can be used again and again." The tin shows
a skating rink scene with many little Brittanys twirling around in
red skating skirts. I enlarge my X, attempting to create the optical
illusion that it fills more than one box. My $7 looks naked and
cheap next to the mostly two-digit figures. Clearly, I hate children.
I replace the catalogue in an interoffice envelope and put it in my
Out Box.

Mine's family has a pet Labrador named Tivoli who has been
diagnosed with obsessive-compulsive disorder. I overhear Mine
discussing the psychological benefits of walking Tivoli in Central
Park after work. He hadn't been in favor of the life decision to get
an animal, but had been railroaded by his daughter. Now it's about

the only downtime he has and he looks forward to it. I try to imagine Mine scooping a loose bowel movement from the sidewalk in the rain into a Baggie or a hunk of the *Wall Street Journal* and I am unable to do it. The dog belongs to a Wellness Plan, a kind of major medical insurance policy with an extremely high deductible that covers things like doggie MRIs and prescription drugs and behavioral therapy with a licensed psychotherapist. Mine asks me to start a separate file for Tivoli and suggests I start processing the claims. Since it's covered by the Wellness Plan, they're thinking of sending Tivoli to a shrink because she has a biting problem. She attacks middle-aged white men in charcoal gray suits and white shirts, carrying folded newspapers.

I have been appointed one of the firm's fire mascots for the thirty-seventh floor and find myself unable to refuse. The disproportionate dread and horror I feel at this responsibility reminds me of when I was asked to help choose teams for sixth-grade kick ball. Dragon Lady asked that I sign up before letting me read what I was getting myself into.

In the event of fire, a floor mascot is required to make sure that everyone is ushered as quickly as possible to the fire exits and told which "hot floors" to avoid. I'm sure I've seen the building's Fire Marshal, with his mottled hound face, at the bar at McFeeley's. I have two fantasies vis-à-vis my role as Fire Mascot. First: I quietly slip away with my backpack and standard issue flashlight the minute I smell a wafting tendril of smoke, take the service elevator to the first floor, and leave everyone to fry. Second: At once more charitable and more grandiose, I herd the Rest-of-Us safely down to a "cool-doored floor," leaving all the Mines, who ignore my instructions, dictating at their desks, which are soon engulfed in flames. When they finally notice and call for me on the intercom, I will not respond. For an entire half-day following my high-rise disaster fantasy, I feel a surge of warmth and benevolence toward the Mines and Almost Mines when they pass by my desk. I have visited mental conflagration upon each and every one of them.

I call home for my messages at least once an hour. My answering machine is switched to Toll Saver so that I hang up after the second ring, unless I hear my own voice, indicating that I have a message. When this happens, my heart always jumps; life may be about to change.

I have recently placed a personal ad in a free downtown newspaper, and have been receiving replies on my voice mail at work. While I have a secret code to access my messages, which no one else can possibly know, I still worry that my phone is secretly hooked into some large office recording bank monitored by Dragon Lady. A blinking envelope symbol in the upper left-hand corner of my phone console effectively introjects my personal life into office business. Mine stands there at my desk jiggling impatiently, not interrupting me only because he assumes that I am engaged in a scheduling interaction on his behalf. In fact, I am listening to a strange man talking. "Hi, there," he says directly into my ear, his voice low and velvety. "Why don't you give me a call? I'd really like to get to know you." Certain messages I keep to listen to again and again, mostly when the voice strokes me right then and there. When I don't like a voice, or when the man says something irredeemably tragic, I take pleasure in hitting the delete code and banishing the voice and the inevitability of a pitiful entanglement out into AT&T limbo. I have not yet called any of these men, but keep a small locked box of index cards on my desk with their phone numbers and a few distinctive details. *Hates movies with subtitles. Joint custody twins, ex-wife lives across street. Cooks Thai.* Sometimes I take the cards out and hold them in one hand in a fan, a poker hand. I'm there with a box full of men on my desk; Mine knows nothing about my life and never chooses to ask.

Mine carries a beeper and a cellular phone in his briefcase. He calls me from his car phone when he's on the highway. I like it that he sounds cut off from the world. "Hello," he shouts, "hello, hello." This could be the first telephone conversation. He writes phone numbers down on a little pad on the dashboard. I hear a CD playing in the background, the New Age dentist's music he likes to drive to. He makes me repeat numbers. He never gets the whole thing the first time. "Just let me pass this one," he always says. This is his way of telling me that he's an exciting driver. I feel sorry for him when he's out of the office. His voice sounds swallowed up, unimportant, especially when he drives into a tunnel or a no-call zone and he disappears in a tidal wave of static. I wonder how my voice sounds coming out of his speaker phone. I get embarrassed calling him in his car when there's an emergency at the office, thinking maybe I'm interrupting something private, he's with his wife or a lover, or eating a Big Mac with fries, dipping a long dangling fry into a tub of ketchup on the seat next to him, or maybe he's pulled off into a rest area and unzipped his fly. Sometimes his wife calls from her car phone while I'm talking to him and he tells me to "patch her in." This involves putting him on hold, calling her back on her car phone and then conferencing the two together by pressing connect and hanging up. This act of facilitation always makes me feel extremely lonely. Mine calls me back and tells me to make dinner reservations.

•   •   •

Everyone takes advantage in some way. No one talks about it. This is being a grown-up. I have over one thousand pens at home, a lifetime collection: turquoise and black ballpoints; black and blue fine felt-tips; pencils, sharpened, unsharpened, snubbed dull; thick yellow and green and dark blue highlighters; Scotch tape without a dispenser; many, many manila folders. I could open a doctor's office. I often try to remember to take pens from home back to the office when my supply there is low, my own private Amnesty Program. Peach hands them out, two by two like methadone. Then I forget and slip a couple into my bag at night and take them home and the cycle starts all over again.

(Note: Federal Express letter envelopes make nice little brief-cases.)

The first time I heard someone throwing up in the ladies' room at work was midmorning. I thought it was Little Pregnant One or Madonna, Esq., or someone who had just come down with flu. I noted the shoes. I worried that I should do something. It happened again a week later, same time, same shoes. Ten-fifteen. Black pumps with a small gold buckle. Rough throwing up, a prolonged gag finale, I could almost feel the forefinger poking at the back of her throat. I figured out who it was later by doing a shoe match. I don't know what to do about this, entertain the idea that there is something I can do, mostly because I know there isn't. This Almost Mine is rail thin, wrists like coat hangers. Yogurt lunches at her desk, always stops at the candy jar and takes handfuls. Word has it she never stops work, a twelve-year-old girl's body, her suits hang. Everyone jokes that she's so nervous she probably makes love holding an escrow agreement behind her husband's shoulder, leaves her tape recorder under her pillow at night, still dictating . . . *Oh, baby, baby, baby, pursuant to my love for you . . .*

.   .   .

I read in a magazine about some things you can do to combat depression:

Get enough sun.

Eat salmon with skin.

Move to the seashore.

Purchase a negative-ion machine.

Perform repetitive motions: chew gum, lick your lips, knit.

Take vitamin C, B6 and melatonin supplements at night.

Eat oatmeal, not cooked in the microwave.

Stand near a waterfall.

On the subway, I close my eyes, chew gum rhythmically, transform the train sounds into a river, imagine a waterfall rushing past my face.

Does typing count?

Mine is going off to Canyon Ranch again next week. He's taking his wife and leaving his daughter and the baby with Milagros, the au pair. She calls the office at least once a day, asking me questions. "This is Milagros," she always says in her stiff English, as though we have never spoken before. I think she resents that I spend so much time with Him, am in some possession of his valuable waking hours. I've never met her, but imagine a small woman with dark hair, impractically long, so that she's always moving it back in a curtain away from the baby's pureed spinach and banana-pear. Mine's eyes will meet hers often, at the breakfast table, over the top of his baby's head and his wife's as she leans over the *Wall Street Journal.* I know that Mine and Au Pair have never made love, but both have thought about it. She thinks him stiff but appreciates the way he arrives home late carrying a great many papers in his briefcase and sits hunched over his tiny notebook computer at the coffee table, his legs spread apart, his expensive wool pants hitched up and pleated brutally at the thighs. She serves him beer in a bottle and a microwaved steak sandwich. Sometimes she makes him her special rice pudding which he finds too sweet, but eats anyway. As she hangs up, Milagros pronounces my name incorrectly with too many syllables.

While Mine is away I enjoy certain freedoms. I screen and then reseal his Confidential mail, take long lunch hours, sit at his desk after work to apply makeup. I close the door and stare out at his view, the lights winking over the river, the bridge arching, the hectic prettiness of the sunset skyline. I browse through his top desk drawer. I prop my mirror against a stack of his papers and lean down into it. There is a knock on the door and I fumble while putting the makeup away, tuck the whole case under my armpit and tiptoe to the door with politely raised eyebrows. It's one of the Almost Thems: *I thought we had a meeting, when is he calling in, it is imperative that I speak to him immediately, give me his hotel number.* I imagine him at Canyon Ranch getting whipped/hosed by one of those large Eastern European women all dressed in white, until his pale back and buttocks are streaked red, and then he'll lie down so that she can beat him with willow branches until he whimpers.

"Incommunicado," I say with the same pretentious pronunciation that Mine uses, rhyming it with staccato. "Incommunicado," I repeat to this frantic Almost Them, backing him out of Mine's office with firm body language and a discreet smile.

*   *   *

Mine's eleven-year-old daughter calls this morning while he's on a conference call. "He can't come to the phone," I tell her.

"I can't wait," she says, "I'm tight for time."

"He can't come to the phone right now."

"I need to know if he can pick me up from my play date tonight."

"He really is unavailable, but I'll give him the message."

"I have to go now. I have another call coming through," she says.

Mine asks me to make reservations for her on a flight to Fort Lauderdale where one of her friends is having a birthday party. He hands me her Delta Frequent Flyer card.

"Can you believe," I overhear Mine boasting on the phone, "she starts every sentence these days with 'To the best of my knowledge.' A lawyer's daughter, or what?"

In terroreum. Ipse dixit. Actus reus. Ad damnum.

The office leash law keeps most of us tethered close by; to disobey it by getting on the subway at lunch hour, for example, and traveling even a few stops, would make the world seem brighter and more potent with guilty possibilities. To venture afield, in the manner of a soldier going AWOL, or someone who has learned that he may die, is a temporary liberation only.

I'm standing next to a bright turquoise subway pillar that has a WET PAINT sign on it. I stroke it with my finger to see if it's really wet, then reach into my pocket with the other hand for a Kleenex. Inside a plastic bag, inside my leather shoulder bag, I'm carrying a sandwich in a Ziploc bag. I double wrap things so that my bag won't stink like a lunch box. Sometimes I forget to make lunch. Often, I'm on my way out, have even closed the door and put my key in the front lock when I remember. Something flashes through my mind about savings and the sad hopelessness of office lunches, the operating room lights over the salad bar, big, dry, expensive sandwiches, salty chicken noodle soup: I'll never get away, never have a house, never be free. I walk back in, still in my jacket, and double-time assemble bread and peanut butter and jelly, or two slices of processed ham and Alpine Lace low-fat cheese, which might as well be plastic, and slap it together, shove it into the corner of a big shopping bag. The thinness of the home-made sandwich, the way peanut butter and jelly and whole wheat bread condense and bleed in the three hours before lunch, has not changed since grade school.

I'm not yet sure where I'm going and when I'm going to eat, a dangerous position to be in on a strict lunch hour.

Sometimes, when I have to take a late lunch, I shop. A department store is best, preferably upscale, with beautiful lighting, expensive fabrics. I browse through women's lingerie, racks of underwear I can't afford. I do this as though I have a life that involves such underwear. I touch a Japanese brown silk bra that costs eighty-five dollars, a tiny filigreed garter belt no wider than a girl's hair ribbon. I try on a low-cut black bra and a cobwebby garter belt. The effect is ruined by my cotton Jockey-for-Hers underneath, I have the look of a pervert, an impostor, stuffing herself into something alien. I pull them off. I practice snapping the garters with one hand, an action from a western saloon scene. I take a seat in the dainty tufted chair in the corner of the dressing room and spread my legs wide, rest my elbow on one knee and lean into my hand, cock my head sideways and look at myself from every angle in the three-paneled mirror. My breasts look large and rounded, unmolded flans. I stick my tongue out and flick it up and down and extend one leg to the right, the other to the left in a semi-aerial, butt-balanced split: a job across the street at Flashdancers, collecting dollars in my underwear, a job as a topless barmaid, a room service waitress, a call girl, an enraged, overqualified, oversized geisha, anything would be better. I get dressed and decide not to buy the bra or the garter belt, hastily coax the fairy-princess straps into the hanger slits, hand them to the woman at the dressing room gate, knowing I am clean, I am broke, I am guilty of this one sin.

I hate eating in the subway. The grease and subway urine smell makes my throat close. Sometimes I walk around the office neighborhood and eat my sandwich right out of my shoulder bag. Dry sandwiches you can eat as you're walking along without receiving too much attention. Walks during lunch hour are crucial for the mental state, also a way to eat without wasting too much time. Occasionally, people look at me strangely, as though I'm a homeless person who's pulled a sandwich out of a trash can. Because of this, I walk and eat only when I'm dressed up, preferably wearing a suit. With my Nikes and white socks and neutral stockings, and the suit and the sandwich, I look like what I'm supposed to be: a secretary multi-tasking on her lunch hour.

The train arrives and I get on and take my favorite place, the downtown corner of the long seat. Pulling in close to the metal armrest, I hook my elbow over it. This way, if someone gets on they're unlikely to stand too close. One of the hazards of this particular seat is that incoming passengers stand sideways so that their buttocks are only one inch away from your head.

My plan is to go two stops and sit for a while in the park, half a block from the train station, eat my sandwich, then return by subway with five minutes to spare so I can buy a good cup of coffee, and still get back in time. This split-second timing is a risk. Today, the doors stay open with no explanation and we sit there sniffing at the smoky smell that rises, animals refusing to leave the barn. A surreal feeling overtakes me, one part paranoia/two parts loneliness. What if I just stayed here and we never moved?

The subway doors finally close and we lurch forward. Before we travel even one station, the train stops and sits, milk train timing. My body is beginning to manufacture stress prickles.

At the park, I sit on one end of a flaking green bench close to the subway entrance, and unwrap my sandwich. After a few minutes, a man in a gray wool overcoat sits down at the other end of my bench and opens his ThinkPad. Placing a brown bag between us, he carefully folds the top down. Both sets of our feet are soon covered in bobbing birds. They seem to know him. One bird cocks its head up at me as though it's plotting to dive up toward my sandwich. I make a lunging motion with one foot and they all fly away, raising dust. I'm worried about his hard drive.

"I beg your pardon," he says, "would you like a grape? Seedless?" He pushes the bag closer toward me on the bench. The grapes are not on their vine but are rolling around loose, as though he bought them at a secondhand shop. They look coated in a dusty haze of pesticides.

"No thank you." My voice sounds sepulchral, never used. Lunch hour is supposed to give us all commonality, sixty minutes of freedom, perfect bonding material.

I take a bite of my sandwich, my taste buds instantly self-conscious, worrying that my homemade tuna smells. I keep taking small bites and swallowing them quickly, until two choppy carved-out crusts are left. I crush the rest of my sandwich into the bag and scrunch it into a ball, feeling the tuna and bread clump and slide, then I stand and brush crumbs from my lap. The birds immediately flock back for this latest snack.

"I have to get back to the office," I say.

"Me too," he says, continuing to type but looking up at me.

"Let's not," I say.

He laughs with his head back, showing some food. I stand there, and he sits there for a minute or two in silence. "Here, take the rest of these," he says, holding up the crumpled bag.

"That's all right, I'm full," I say.

He presses the bag of grapes against my arm. "No, really, take them."

"Thanks," I say, taking the bag, already planning at which corner I'll toss out the sour, chemically things. I pause as I leave, glancing back, wondering whether he will call out something, ask for my e-mail address, but his head is already bent toward his computer.

Back in the subway, aimlessness soon overpowers the AWOL adrenaline and underscores the fact that my job isn't important at all. If I were to disappear, by the next day another temp would fill my chair and by the following week, most certainly a permanent replacement. How long would Mine pause to ruminate on any tragedy that might befall me, say, if I were to be shoved under the oncoming subway by the guy who's standing over by the pillar, muttering? I have wondered about this many times, through various scenarios, in a dispassionate, unself-pitying fashion. I see Mine for a single moment glancing on the fleeting nature of relationship (a single deep thought, a leftover from a course in existentialism he took in college). There is some relief in knowing that I am so replaceable, that if I were to choose not to return from lunch, nothing much would really happen.

．   ．   ．

With three minutes to spare, I'm standing in line for coffee, which is taking way too long, but I take the risk anyway, unable to imagine how I will get through the rest of the afternoon without a strong cup. I pray that people will want old-fashioned brew. No one says "coffee regular" anymore. The man in front of me orders "a double half-caff mocha two-percent latte with a sip-top lid" from the young man with Greta Garbo eyebrows. I watch the espresso machine ballet, try not to dance with impatience.

"Next," says Greta Garbo in a sultry, gruff voice.

"Regular coffee," I say.

The eyebrows go up, mock disdain.

Office coffee remains the old joke, thin, metallic and head-achey. None of Them seem to notice that they are drinking poison. I spend far too much money each week for my dark brown drug. It sits and grows cold at my desk, then I push it back to join the day's collection of containers, the sip-top lids marked with different colors of lipstick, depending on my mood each hour. I drink it later that afternoon, room temperature and slightly scummed, an addiction, only the Cleaning Angel really knows.

Garbo slides a cardboard anti-lawsuit cuff over my hot cup, and I donate my change to his tip cup. "Have a good afternoon," he says, raising one gingerbread-colored brow.

This afternoon I allow myself a passing comfort, I feel warm and open and for a brief moment part of a family. Mine comes out of his office and jokes with me, I feel the blush rising from my chest, relentlessly, toward my face. I rest my cheek in my hand so he won't notice, feel the stain spilling outside my fingers and up toward my forehead, watch him pull away, see it in his eyes, and then he literally backs away. He sees that the attention means something to me. I notice that he feels the warning signals, he's treating me too much like wife/daughter/friend, it's time to back off now. He takes his papers and abruptly turns away. I leave my hand over my face like a bandage, type with my left hand for half a page, pretending to myself that nothing at all has happened, which is actually the case.

The non-dissolving party grants its prior written consent to such dissolution, merger or consolidation and the successor expressly assumes in writing such dissolving . . .

I've recently read that if you commit a violent crime in your sleep, you're not legally accountable for your actions. During this sleep-related violence, a part of the brain wakes up, just enough to allow you to perform some complex act without intent, awareness or malice while the rest of you innocently sleeps. On waking up, you are horrified. As a child, I used to sleepwalk. Coming downstairs in the night, I would turn on the television, tune into a program and switch channels. Once I walked outside and turned down the street, returning with a bouquet of flowers picked from different neighbors' gardens, which I handed to my mother. After a night of overtime, or when typing a very long and boring document, I have sometimes nodded off at the terminal. I imagine myself walking into Mine's office in this state, smashing all of his framed degrees over his head, one by one, so that they form a thick angular necklace around his neck, then returning to my desk, innocent. Victims of this sleep affliction are likely to be people with haphazard sleep schedules (overtime/night shifts), or who have experienced recent distressing events, or who consume a great deal of caffeine.

●   ●   ●

Dragon Lady makes the rounds of the corral commandeering overtime volunteers. It's for a not-bad Mine with manageable handwriting who smokes cigarettes and listens to the radio after eight o'clock. Once every two weeks or so I do overtime, only if I can put in enough hours to assure myself a ride home and a free dinner. Some of the others stay every night, a fatally bad habit, fostering a false sense of importance that comes along with sprawling in the backseat of a shiny black, numbered town car night after night, with no exchange of cash.

The central air shuts off after eight o'clock, creating a sudden, eerie stillness. Within minutes, the air is voluptuously stuffy. We take off our shoes, turn on radios. We order Chinese food, fried dumplings and sesame noodles and shredded pork with garlic sauce and slide the cartons up and down the long, slick conference room table. Sometimes a few of Them will join the Rest-of-Us, standing behind our chairs, grabbing for the cartons, one eating straight from them with chopsticks, a misguided way to break plantation ranks.

I have trouble holding on to reality. I feel both more comfortable, as though a bathrobe is not far away, and panicky as the office empties out and the quiet thickens, thinking about fires and high-rise rapists and plummeting elevators. Outside the night is ultra black with pretty firefly lights in neighboring buildings, a helicopter's-eye view. Inside, the light changes and with fewer bodies, desks loom. Xeroxing seems illicit. My cubicle is illuminated differently, reminding me of my father's study. Greater involvement in the world seems possible after hours, an illusion created by the shifting of power. If we chose to, we could plunder their offices, sabotage the network, scrawl lipstick across the art deco mirror in reception, cut up the carpets, but we don't.

This is my fantasy. It's after hours and a slow overtime night; the office is dead except for Mine, who's still sitting there talking into his dictaphone. I walk up behind him holding a strong piece of black silk cord. I hold it wrapped around both hands and pressed against my chest. I make sure that his arms are down at his sides as I begin to lift the cord. Before he has time to react, I wrap it around him twice, three times, and continue to wind it around the base of the chair, back and forth, intricate as a spider's web. I ignore his spluttering and swearing. "You'll pay for this," he keeps saying. There's spit on his chin. I unplug the receiver from the phone, wrap it with the cord and drop it into the wastebasket. I wipe the spit from his chin with my hand. I set the dictaphone carefully on the desk in front of him, and press Record. Turning out the lights, I leave, closing the door, and listen for a moment. He has already begun to speak.

Assuming arguendo, I type, *I have the authority to bind.*

At the end of the night I change clothes in Mine's office. I lock the door and turn out the lights. The building across the street suddenly leaps closer as though the houselights have been turned down for a play. I drop my skirt and peel off my stockings and underpants, step out of them by doing a couple of marching steps, stretching to pull off the feet, and kick them across the office so they land on the piled-up papers on Mine's credenza. I sit on his chair to unbutton my blouse, then toss it across the desk so that it lands on my dictation chair. Leaning back, I swivel slightly, enjoying the cool leather up and down my bare back. I squirm a little on the seat. I know this isn't grown-up. The wife is half-facing me, her teeth and the snows of Vail gleaming bright in the shadowy office. I turn the picture so that she faces me directly.

"Good evening," I say. She looks at me speculatively, her eyes glinting. "Your husband's a prick."

I call the weather, then Dial-A-Car. It's almost midnight, but the place sounds like a full-service garage at noon. The operator puts me on hold for five minutes and plays the theme from *Rocky* in my ear. I switch to hands-free and swivel in place in the chair for another minute or two. The dispatcher interrupts. Car number 435 will be waiting downstairs in ten minutes. Still sitting in the chair, I pull my sweatpants from my bag and yank them on, leg by leg, without underwear, then an old T-shirt and a pair of beat-up moccasins. It's important for me to leave at night almost ready for bed. I open his one unlocked drawer and place his wife, face-down, on top of a raft of his favorite fine-point pens, and close the drawer. If he asks, it was Cleaning Angel. I stuff my balled-up tights and underwear into my bag. At the door, I turn on the lights for a split second, long enough to see the faint seashell outline of myself on my boss's champagne leather chair.

Owl, the night word processor kisses me good night on both cheeks. He's in the middle of a ten-page table, fifteen columns of decimal tabs, his brow furrowed in concentration.

"Home safe," he says, not looking up.

Just for a second, I consider staying all night, curled up under the desk next to him. "Jesus, girl, get a life," I can hear Owl saying, rolling his big dark eyes in disgust.

Waiting at the elevator bank, I watch Jose polishing the floor in his dark blue maintenance uniform with his name stitched in spidery sixth-grade script on the breast pocket. Waving at me, he leaves the machine on and walks away. The floor buffer starts doing its sexy, sideways hula toward me.

Waving in the direction of Jose's back (*Good night! May I please come home with you?*), I get into the elevator. Holding my breath, an OT superstition, I watch the lights move from 37 down to 18 behind the grid at the top of the elevator, daring it to stop or hesitate in its fluid glide, then endure the remaining unlighted floors, trusting that the silent rushing is taking me down and out, although home is not really where I want to be.

I try to plan my haircuts so that there is at least a weekend between the cut and my reappearance at the office. This gives my hair a chance to get over the shock.

Although you say to yourself that none of this matters, this is a lie. Junior high school cafeteria critics have nothing on a vigilant office at 9:05 A.M., ready to sniff out scandal—a hickey, a tight skirt, a piercingly visible hangover—and spread it around.

Mine goes out for haircuts during his lunch hour, comes back looking like a shaved ram and stands at my desk going through the mail in his In Box as though nothing is different. I never know whether to acknowledge the haircut by saying, "I like your haircut," even when I don't. Just to say, "You got a haircut," with no prettying judgment, seems rude. He never appears to need a response anyway, men are like that, not requiring the reassurances women do. Many of Them go to the same salon, and return with the Mine Cut, neat, Marine-naped, completely unsexy. I wonder if he enjoys getting his hair washed. I see him with his neck arched back, his Adam's apple exposed, gulping. Maybe it's the kind of salon where they do Eastern things to the scalp, move down the neck with delicate knuckles, he'll get a twinge down there. The important thing is to get back to work. Shampoo Girl helps him sit up, leans his head and shoulders forward and covers his head with a small white towel, rubs briskly. He pulls away, worried about male pattern balding. His head looks small and scraggly. He tips her well, folding bills into a thin, damp matchstick, which he tucks deep into the pocket of her smock.

Getting a new hair color is even worse than a haircut, especially if you sit under fluorescent lights seven-hours-plus a day. At home, manically wide awake at two in the morning, my shoulders aching from typing sixty pages in less than three hours, I apply Clairol's Tawny Breeze (permanent) to my hair. I stand under the overhead light in my bathroom and remove the towel, let it drape wet around my neck, a drenched boxer. The crown of my head is surrealy burnished, pulsating chemicals. I go to bed this way, knowing full well that I will wake in the morning to full-blown inmate hair, stuck up in a jagged point on top, the sides flattened and greasy with bad dreams.

On a tightrope, stuck midweek, lurching toward the opposite platform.

In the middle of the night I wake up, remembering that I forgot to send a package by Federal Express. I visualize it sitting there at the back of my desk where I shoved it late in the afternoon to keep it away from my coffee. I bolt up in bed, head automatically for the bathroom, for one wild moment imagine getting dressed and taking a cab to the office, sneaking upstairs, retrieving the package, coming on to an off-duty Fed Ex man, or taking the first flight to Dallas myself in navy blue shorts. The only way I can fall back to sleep is by deciding I'll call in sick in the morning, then never go back to the office.

Once I forgot to place the order for an important client breakfast. This fact infiltrated my dreams the night before. In the dream
I carried a huge tray of cakes and cookies and muffins that kept
rolling off the tray and into doorways. I couldn't sleep for the rest
of the night. I arrived at the office an hour ahead of time and called
the Mad Muffin, requesting a rush delivery. "That's impossible.
We're very backed up," the woman said in a bored voice. "Please,"
I begged, "this is an emergency. Someone has died. It's for a
funeral breakfast." I closed my eyes as I said this, cringing at the
grade school–level blurt. I heard a thick, scornful silence on the
other end. My sanity and self-respect, my future, lay with ten
muffins cut in half vertically and two-point-five pounds of fruit
salad.

"Please, please, please," I said in a broken voice. I wanted to
offer to do something for her, to plug her meter, to take her to
dinner. "Well, all right," she said finally. "But only this once." I felt
so warmly grateful, I almost came.

THURSDAY

THERE IS AN ART TO CALLING IN SICK. THE POSSIBILITY enters my mind the night before, fleetingly. *Maybe I'll call in sick tomorrow.* This works its way through my dreams all night. Like most conscientious employees, I resent using sick days when I am actually sick.

I set the alarm for the usual time and wake early, seconds before it goes off. Lying in bed, I test my ability to pull off the deception. If my mind stays blank when I try to do my usual mental fashion show, that's a clue. If I can't imagine myself sumo wrestling onto the subway, it means I don't have the fight to go into work.

I clear my throat. A hint of thickness there, definitely sore. Mostly, it's the orange hair.

I set the alarm for an hour later, too late to make it into the office on time. The die is cast. I fall back to sleep. I dream about calling in sick and wake to the alarm, confused as to whether I've actually done this. At two minutes after eight, when Call Girl comes on duty, I hang upside down over the edge of my bed, allowing fluids to pool inside my head and throat. I'm careful not to clear my throat the whole time the phone is ringing, so that she will get the full, thick benefit. I talk to her lying upside down. Identifying myself, I mumble, "I'm sick." "You sound terrible," she says. Part of her job is to spy for Dragon Lady: "She's really sick; he's faking it."

Euphoria sets in. I've been successful. I prance through my apartment in socks. I study the way the sun progresses across the furniture. I recklessly seize on home decorating ideas, grab a picture and start pounding a nail into the wall in a new place, just as quickly give up. I eat three pieces of toast with butter and honey and drink two cups of coffee on a tray in bed and then fall asleep again and dream that I start to go to work and fall down on the way and have to come back, my stockings ripped and dirty. When I wake up I'm disoriented and can't tell for a while if this actually happened. I go into my bathroom to see if there is a muddy torn pair of stockings in front of the toilet where I sometimes leave them, two tired donuts. I eat another breakfast, consume three more during the course of the day. By the end of the day, I've eaten nine pieces of toast.

For the first few hours, I lie around, dreading discovery. In my semiprivate (unlocked) desk drawer at work are months of phone and credit card bills, annotated pages from the personals, torn-out newspaper clippings about murders and self-help books, canceled checks, a seed catalogue, an Eve's Garden catalogue, a horoscope chart, a personalized fitness program, a bag of pecan granola tied with a twisted paper clip, a letter from an old boyfriend describing oral sex in his car, a sports bra, a sunglasses repair kit, a solar calculator, a pass offering a free tango lesson at Fred Astaire Dance Studio. The perfect desk for a serial killer, a postal worker, a spy

disguising her traces in a manic paper trail. All these things spread
out on the police detective's desk. He would shake his head and
say, 'Who knew her?'

I spend the whole afternoon worrying about whether to call in
sick again the next day. I am a proponent of the piggyback theory,
which says that if you're guilty about being out one day you might
as well be out two, if not three; it's more authentic, fast forward to
bubonic plague. I go out for exactly ten minutes in the afternoon
and rush home, convinced Dragon Lady will have called, leaving
her suspicious voice on my answering machine. *"Are you there?"* I
put my bathrobe back on and lie down, my head over the edge
upside down, waiting, feeling authentically feverish, stockpiling
phlegm. "I still have a fever," I experiment, my voice breaking
pathetically. No one calls. For the next hour I tingle with guilt.
After five I pour myself a glass of wine, feeling let down. Sick days
always confirm your worst fear/favorite fantasy: They don't really
need you.

It's important to go into the office the next morning not
wearing any lipstick or eye makeup. While the reaction is ego-
damaging, authenticity is key. Cosmetic color can be restored by
noon.

FRIDAY

T.G.I.F. PEOPLE REALLY DO SAY THIS.

I suffer from Casual Day Anxiety. This one day a week of corporate slumming is supposed to make us feel informal, nonchalant, relaxed, the Thems and Almost Thems joining the slaves for a watermelon party. I have no wish to impress, simply to pass. To allow us to type documents in blue jeans is to offer us liberation. On these Friday mornings I pull everything I own from my closet and drawers and just as quickly discard them, leaving a three-foot mountain on my bed. Casual Day clothes are not what you'd pull out of your bottom drawer on Saturday morning to run out and buy a bagel.

The list of things to be afraid of while commuting grows every day. Sitting on the subway on the way to work, maybe I'll get jabbed with a hypodermic needle and contract Hepatitis B or H.I.V., or maybe there'll be someone in my car with a gun hidden in a jacket, or a homemade bomb made out of a mayonnaise jar, or maybe I'll get stuck in the train and suffer smoke inhalation because of a track fire. Funny, I don't think about those things when actually commuting, just loll, often peacefully, as though the seat is an extension of my bed, that core of warmth right inside, I fall asleep over the paper, enjoying my coffee breath. I can tell certain fellow passengers do the same thing, lean against each other, oddly trusting.

Before work, I go to a palm reader/adviser I've noticed on my lunch hour. I saw her sign in the window on a side street I hadn't been down before. Sometimes when you cover a lot of blocks and pass by different neighborhoods, the hour seems longer than an hour. I like seeing people sitting on their stoops and yelling out the windows of their apartments during my day at the office. You can find all the life you need just a few blocks west. I buy a second paper at a corner bodega just to hear the woman call me sweetie in her Spanish accent. Even early in the morning, it smells good over there, meat and garlic.

I stand outside looking up at the sign. A woman pushes back the gauzy pink curtain and beckons me to come inside. I shake my head no, but keep standing there, undecided. She holds up five fingers twice and points to them and smiles. Her teeth are white and even and there's a graceful wing-shaped shadow of hair on her upper lip. A magenta blouse pulls over large, soft-looking breasts. I walk up the patched cement stairs. She's sitting on a low couch. She gestures to a chair opposite her, and pours a half-cup of sweet coffee from a black carafe and tells me to drink it, then takes the cup from me. She stares down into it, studying my dregs. "Man trouble," she says, *"Si?"*

"Si," I say, thinking of Mine sitting at his desk, losing his train of thought.

She tells me to go home, tear two pieces from a brown paper bag and write my name on one, the man's name on the other, crumple them up and put them both together into a jar of honey. This will sweeten the relationship. I pay her ten dollars and she squeezes my hand and pats my cheek and shakes her head, looking sad. I give her ten more.

The fashion parade begins as Mine stands at my desk this morning, the collar of his yellow alligator Lacoste shirt tweaked up to his ears, his forearms exposed and frail-looking, the hairs raised in startled definition around his watchband. We talk as though we are naked, avoiding each other's eyes. Mine's clothes speak of weekend country gentry with a sad city twist. Once he wore jeans, the front ironed to knife pleats and a pair of cowboy boots, the chestnut brown toes aggressively tip-tilted like the prows of speedboats. He walked down the hall stiffly, as though his thighs were chafed. I waited for him to slip on the carpeting. I longed to pull the boots from his feet, to leave him at his desk in his socks, to take the boots outside and scuff them up. He was the laughingstock that day, Midnight Cowboy, the Casual Day casualty.

I can no longer postpone the intimacy of getting up and turning my back to him in order to face the printer. Not too tight, not too faded, my Levi's are especially bought for this enforced relaxation, my shirt carefully ironed and tucked in. I know his eyes are there, for a split-second, on my Casual Day derriere.

Mine and the Biggest Mine are standing in front of my desk arguing. They're both turning red, the color creeping up their necks slowly, roosters facing off. Mine's legs are twitching a mile a minute, I can tell by the movement of his waist, just visible over the top of my desk, subtle yet frantic. Almost imperceptibly, he starts moving back one step, then a long wait, another step, feet together, gradually trying to edge the enemy back toward his lair. BM doesn't budge, stands there with his arms crossed, his glasses held in one hand, shoulders squared off. Neither seems to notice or care that I am three feet away, shuffling papers.

"What is this, Amateur Hour?" BM says, hitting the document he's holding with the back of his hand against his leg.

Mine doesn't say anything. I'm praying for the phone to ring. Not so much to save him, but I can taste a game of Kick the Slave/Kick the Dog in my future. BM walks away and Mine goes into his office, slams the door. I stare at the phone, anticipating my cue. When the intercom buzzes, sharp as a hornet, I jump anyway. "Come in," he says, clipped, ferocious. I gather my pad and spend a while panicking, fumble around in my pen caddy for a sharp enough pencil, picking up one and staring blankly at the point, picking up another, then a third, stalling, unable to find the perfect weapon.

He's sitting there with his feet crossed up on his desk leaning back in his chair, his Big Man on Campus pose. "Let's get some work done," he says, bringing his chair crashing down on the Plexiglas carpet protector.

I sit down with hemorrhoidal care and stare down at my pad. Whether I bark, meow or caw, I'm going to get kicked. He makes me recite his calendar for the following week. I can't remember next Tuesday. I have to get up in the middle to retrieve his large desk calendar, which sits on a special desk across the room. He frowns and drums his fingers impatiently on the arms of his chair, a deranged, furious beat. I sit down again. I turn the pages slowly. I try to speak soothingly. He has four meetings on Tuesday and a Republican fund-raiser in the evening. "Make a note to bring my tux," he says. "Tux," I write on a Post-It and stick it to the back of my hand.

. . .

The complainant avers that the plaintiff is being treated in an arbitrary, capricious, discriminatory and predatory fashion.

I know this to be true.

There are things you want to say out loud, but don't, office Tourette's. Mine strides purposefully down the hall, slapping his thigh with *Crain's New York Business Week* rolled into a dog swatter. I watch him the whole way, knowing he will veer in entitled fashion into the men's room. Reading material is carried boldly by men. Here, there and everywhere, they do big business. Women never do this. It's not that we don't read. It's something to do with our toilet training. We carry our papers and magazines and novels hidden in our bags, take them out once safely inside a stall, careful not to turn pages too aggressively. Perhaps the men discuss clients stall-to-stall. We daydream, think too much, call out to a familiar pair of shoes, as long as the coast is clear.

Fifteen minutes later Mine strolls out of the men's room. He walks toward his office, humming lightly, doing the post-business power swat with his magazine, hitting first his leg, then briskly each desktop as he passes by.

He whacks my desk and disappears into his office. "Partner goes poop," I singsong under my breath.

It could happen here. His silver-plated letter opener. Tainted tortellini salad. Rat poison in his latte. The Twinkie defense backfires. Twenty-five to life, no hope of parole. Prison librarian, good place to study law. I'll miss cappuccino.

Demands for arbitration on behalf of the grievant have been withdrawn with prejudice.

.   .   .

Automatic deposit is a miracle. When I call the bank and listen to my computerized balance, I feel so full and grateful, I want to kiss Mine, as though he has personally pulled wads of cash from his pockets and handed them to me.

I process Mine's expense receipts today, a monthly task I enjoy because it allows me a fully sanctioned opportunity to spy. He seems to have no idea how much of his life I am able to piece together simply by looking at the small, folded scraps of paper that he pulls from his shirt pocket once a week and hands to me. Occasionally his personal receipts are mixed in by mistake. Yesterday I found an ATM receipt showing a checking account balance of $29,352.06. I stare at this figure for a very long time, try to reconcile it with my own ATM receipt from the same day, showing a balance of –$21.21. I line up the two receipts so that the printed sides face each other, then tear them both up into tiny pieces and flutter them into the wastebasket, an old Eastern blending ritual.

Normally I separate Mine's personal papers and place them discreetly in an envelope, ready should he ever ask for them. Mostly they're receipts for weekend dinners at suburban restaurants, CDs charged for his daughter, dry cleaner bills, prescriptions for his high blood pressure medication. In an odd, deprived way, I relish this personal scrapbook. I particularly enjoy it when Mine has taken an out-of-town business trip. With the newly detailed computer receipts, I am able to see an itemized list of what he has eaten and drunk. Last week, for example, on an overnight trip to Washington, D.C., he dined alone at his hotel, consuming half a dozen bluepoint oysters, Lobster Thermidor, two Amstel Light beers, a piece of mocha cheesecake, and a decaf cappuccino.

Who orders Lobster Thermidor? Who orders Lobster Thermidor alone? This meal took place at 8:05 and was served by waiter No. 11. I see Mine sitting at the back curve of a round table, exhausted, elbows on the snowy cloth, his square briefcase open on the booth next to him like a traveling salesman. I am surprised that he likes raw oysters and drinks beer. I wonder if his thoughts ever drift to me when he's alone. While this tableside picture is quite vivid, it becomes fuzzy and vague when I try to follow him upstairs and down the hall to his hotel room. I am fully capable of imagining myself, however, dressed in a long black dress with a thigh-high slit and my new Raisin Rage lipstick, standing at his door, about to knock. This fantasy has less to do with sexual desire than it does with a wish to catch him in some out-of-town indiscretion, the counselor-at-law who likes to be spanked like a naughty schoolboy while wearing nothing but his black lawyer's socks.

An hour later I have written out my bills and realize that I have forty-five dollars to live on until my next automatic deposit in two weeks. A sullen teenager again, I slump in my chair. I think about all of Mine's offshore accounts, his investments, his kids' trust funds, his wife's charge accounts, his imported wine account at Sherry-Lehmann, his brie and arugula sandwiches, his Barney's ties. I have a piggybank life with a savings account closed for inactivity, hard-boiled egg and saltines again for lunch.

On her last day, Little Pregnant One comes to work wearing stretch pants and a blazingly white sweatshirt that says *Look What We Made* in big black letters. Dragon Lady calls her into her office to tell her she's dressed inappropriately. "This belly and this butt are too big for those clothes and for these people," Little Pregnant One says. After she's had the baby, we're going to look into how she can sue for retroactive maternity benefits, especially if they don't hire her back. They're still trying to figure out a maternity leave policy for the support staff, although the plan for all the Mines is firmly in place.

Her mother comes in around lunchtime for the baby shower carrying a cake on a tinfoil tray, and a miniature blue plastic bassinet stuck in the frosting. Little Pregnant One unwraps the collapsible stroller and stack of baby blankets and she and her mother both cry. We put them in a cab back uptown and I give the driver ten dollars. Little Pregnant One leans out of the cab as we stand on the sidewalk watching. Her long black hair flies out and sprays against the yellow taxi. "They can go fuck themselves," she yells back. Her mother leans over, trying to pull her back inside.

He doesn't fuck me, feed me or pay my rent. We say this at work with a hand on one hip, a few curse words and flying saliva, our Mines out of hearing range. The first point is true in most cases, the second and third points are actually not, the reason that most of us aren't free.

Every office has one person you most don't want to end up like. Accounts Payable is an aging beauty queen who found herself on the accounting treadmill. Her big dream is to relocate to Atlantic City. Every other weekend she gambles on the nickel slot machines. Her job involves a never-ending pile of expense receipts, many of them from take-out deliveries and covered in grease, particularly the ones from Chinese restaurants. "By now I can pick out the garlic sauce," she says. Once a week she calls up Tea Den and yells at the manager for writing their bills in Chinese.

Even though I gave up smoking years ago, I go downstairs with AP and we smoke cigarettes together. We slouch against a pillar, our knees buckling occasionally, part of the sullen cigarette culture. I smoke the way she does, pulling hard, our cheeks caved in like Lauren Bacall's. In daylight, her makeup is pancake thick, her brown eyes tragically bloodshot, still beautiful. She tells me about her recent ingrown toenail operation. "I wore high heels for too many years," she says, squinting with a passionately long look down the street. "Now I have to wear these." She thrusts one foot out in her flat, spongy-soled shoe, allowing ash to sprinkle down. Every day we talk about her shoes.

Mine hands me a stapled document and asks for five copies, immediately. He's in a meeting. Through the half-opened door I can see the Visiting Mines sitting around his table by the window, their legs crossed, yellow pads scattered across the table. I take the ten-page oversized chart and wrestle the industrial staple out of the corner, leaving the edges of the paper slightly torn and bent. Frantic, I curl the corners back and forth, smoothing them out. My professional analysis of the job: double-sided, collated, stapled, reduced. I press all the right buttons on the Xerox machine and stick the pages in and walk away. The first copy goes safely through, then I hear the machine jamming, the hopeless whirring sound of paper hitting the guardrail. I return to the scene and begin pulling out casualties. The showcase first page of the original document is an accordion-pleated disaster. The other pages are now rushing for the exit as well, the machine spewing them out upside down, monstrously disordered. I notice the pages aren't numbered. "The world is not ending," I say to myself as my heartbeat accelerates. I take the only good copy and the reamed original and go back to my desk. Sitting down, I brace myself with a sip of cold coffee. Through the crack in the office door I can see Mine pacing back and forth; he needs his visual prop, the accident in my lap. I kneel on the floor behind my desk and spread out the pages, turn them upside down and back to front, and with a terrible calm, determine a new order, reminding myself that people only pretend to read spreadsheets. Back at the machine I hand-feed them through, one by one, defying the Xerox poltergeist. I carry the copies into his office. Not looking at me, he grabs them. One of the VMs leers at me, holding up his coffee cup.

Mine looks up at me.

"Would you mind?" he says.

"Milk, sugar, Sweet'n Low?" I ask, not quite doing the Playboy bunny dip.

More often than not, you type a sixty-page document and at the end of it you have no idea what you've typed. The Mines don't understand this brain phenomenon. They think you simply have no capacity. *It would make your job more interesting, wouldn't it?* their look says. If you don't believe this, try duplicating in your head the letters on the middle row of the keyboard. You may have been typing a hundred words a minute for twenty years and still be unable to do this, which explains why it is possible to type so many pages without absorbing anything. This statement is a testament to the lengths to which the brain will go to protect itself from unwanted information. As Mine never deigns to ask my opinion on a brief or an agreement, or a particularly spectacular example of legal blabbage, I am rarely faced with this problem. Mine spends all day making small changes on long documents: commas, tenses, connecting words, phrasing, fiddling self-importantly with boilerplate. I've always resented it when he asks me to witness a legal document, knowing that it means nothing, that my name, address and signature will appear at the bottom of a sheaf of pages I have not been asked to read. "What am I signing?" I imagine saying as I scrawl my name on the signature line. I picture his incredulous look, the contemptuous rise in his eyebrow at this evidence of pride, the way he would turn on his heel and simply move on to another of the Rest-of-Us. To ask what's really going on at the office, would be like asking your parents if they have oral sex.

Sometimes they spring sudden big changes on us, afraid we'll subvert the process if given any warning. You try to make each workstation a home-away-from-home the way you're supposed to, but then you have to pick up and leave. A new identity, last minute, the Witness Protection Program. Lately the whole list comes by e-mail. *New Desk Assignments* the heading reads. *The following secretaries will be relocated and will work for:* fill in the blank. You're given a cardboard box and told to move the things from your desk, like changing cubicles at a homeless shelter. People have to pull down the pictures of their loved ones, careful not to rip the face off a husband or son. We look forlorn, carrying boxes of personal possessions. It's like transferring to another jail, your whole life in one cardboard box. This game of musical chairs leaves everyone bruised. Your neighbor, the one you discussed last night's date with every morning, is now down the hall. You stop by the new desk and visit over the back fence, but she now lives in a different neighborhood, with alien turf rules. Soon you're awkward when you try to chat, the thing that happens to lovers after they break up. You hate the smell of your new neighbor's perfume.

"This is really scary," Mine says when things go wrong. He says this when I can't find a phone number right away, or when there's a mistake in a document that he didn't notice, and I didn't notice, and it went out to the client that way. He says this standing at my desk holding the document in his hand and looking down at it and shaking his head, then looking at me, then down again as though this will change the embarrassing outcome. "This is really scary," he repeats. I don't know what he wants me to say. I want to say, that's not scary, scary is getting stuck in an elevator during a fire, scary is kids begging in the subway, scary is working for you. I don't know what he expects. He looks at me sorrowfully, right in the eyes, as though I'm supposed to start whimpering, lie down and curl up at his feet, show him my genitals. I shrug then, I don't mean to, it just happens, my body does it independently. When my shoulders are up around my ears I try to turn the motion into something else, dip my ear into my shoulder as though this was all an elaborate attempt to scratch my ear. Then I bring my shoulders down slowly, one at a time, turning away from him toward my computer and playing with the keys, shifting screens a few times, now you see it/now you don't. Finally, he walks away, still carrying the document, shaking his head. Soon he'll be back with the same document and he'll say the same thing again until finally I'll apologize just to make him go away.

Mine calls me from the large conference room. He's sitting at the green marble table with twelve enormous real estate moguls in gray suits. They're all leaning back in their chairs with their jackets open, airing big bellies. These are the clients who always want to order from the expensive deli around the corner. I can tell Mine disapproves. He likes ordering from the even more expensive trattoria twenty blocks away that has smoked turkey and eggplant sandwiches served with a dainty mesclun salad dressed in balsamic vinaigrette. I think he likes the idea of a man in a red waiter's jacket walking quickly along the avenue balancing a tray with his sandwiches, a gentlemen's circus.

When I walk in, they're taking a break. I stand at the end of the conference table fanning my pad of yellow Post-Its, pen ready.

They keep talking. I keep clearing my throat, *ahem,* until finally, they order. Six corned beef sandwiches, six hot pastrami sandwiches, extra potato salad, extra pickles, extra coleslaw. A plate of cookies. *Oh, wait, Miss, extra mustard. Extra napkins.* I'm a waitress again. I call in the order by phone, putting it on Mine's corporate American Express, order one extra corned beef sandwich for myself that will get lost in the crowd. When the order comes, I stash my sandwich inside a manila envelope and stow it in my drawer. I bring everything else into the conference room on a big tray and leave it in the middle of the table. They all look up at me, as though tip size is on their minds.

Leaving, I pause with my tray down at my side and watch through the frosted glass doors as an octopus of gray arms attacks the plate at the center of the table. Why is it that men who order big dripping meat sandwiches always wear plain white shirts? In the kitchen, I furtively triple-wrap my sandwich in tin foil, then paper towels, cut two pickles up and push them into a cardboard coffee cup, slop some coleslaw into another coffee cup. The sandwiches are three inches thick. This will be my dinner for two nights, smuggled out of the office and out of the building, my backpack stinking of pickling spices. Top-of-the-line perks. Ms. Brine 1997.

Super-Step Gym has opened just two blocks from the office. A woman wearing a tight pink workout outfit and a whistle around her neck has been handing out flyers offering a free class. The offer expires today. To save time, I change clothes in the ladies' room at the office, hanging my skirt, blouse and stockings on the back of the stall door as if I'm home in my bathroom and about to jump into the shower. I stand there naked for a few minutes, scratching my stomach, the tiles cool and clammy under my feet. I have the urge to leave the ladies' room, stroll around the corral that way, instant nudist colony.

A pair of feet comes in and sits next to me before I can finish dressing. Quickly, I pull on my iron-maiden sports bra, leotard and tights, then my skirt over my shorts, careful to make all activity occur above bottom-of-the-stall level. I realize I look way too bulky around the middle and remove the shorts and stuff my underpants into the pocket of the shorts, roll them into a tight ball, worried that I will drop them in the hall by mistake and someone will come chasing after me, dangling them on a forefinger. I stalk my way to the elevators, do toe lifts on the way down, calves burning already. From my aerial view I note the faint under-desk dust visible in the eyelets of my aerobic shoes.

At the gym they want to give me a tour. I tell them I'm on my lunch hour. A young woman in a purple warm-up suit sitting behind a desk eating a Danish is still spouting membership deals as she waves me toward the locker room. I choose an out-of-the-way locker and slip out of my corporate disguise, stuff my bag in and quickly slam the door with my hip to keep it all inside, tangle the key safely in my shoelace.

We're doing this forward and backward step over and over again. The teacher, a tiny wiry guy wearing a headset so that his breathy miked voice fills the room, keeps chanting, *rock that pony, turn that pony, ride that pony home.* Fifty women in thong leotards and two progressive businessmen types in corporate-logo sweats are tossing their heads up and down, pawing at the ground, their hands up at waist level as though flicking reins. Halfway through the class, my face is the color of a summer tomato and the hair on the back of my neck is drenched and spiky.

I keep glancing at my watch and losing concentration. In exactly eight minutes I must be sitting behind my desk, composed and dressed, reaching for the phone. Even as I'm rocking back and forth, sweat dripping down between my breasts, a strange, pleasurable inertia overcomes me.

In the middle of Round the World, Pony-Teacher comes up to me and grabs both my hands. Without using my arms for balance, I have to keep my feet moving, stepping up and down on both sides of the step. "Hallelujah," he croons into his headset. "Hallelujah. These steps shall set you free. Amen." He pirouettes away, cackling. The whole class applauds in unison with their stomping feet.

After class I don't bother changing, just layer my work clothes on and jog back to the office, the blood in my face still beating time. This pony is going to get fired.

On Friday afternoon Temp calls her machine one last time. She got the understudy job. The role calls for a fortyish, heavyset bitch goddess. Now she can resume serious carbo-loading. "Dough is my downfall," she says. We exchange numbers. Her card is blowzy and dramatic, the letters bright purple: AEA, SAG, AFTRA. We vow to keep in touch. I write down my work number on a Post-It. She hugs me. I feel relief, repulsion, abandonment. Although I've promised to come and see her in the play, I know I'll never set eyes on her again.

Late on Friday afternoon, they fire Born Again. It happens the way it always does. Fast, before the pig chosen for slaughter can wreck the sty.

Dragon Lady's door is firmly, brutally closed with a different look than it has when it is closed simply for privacy. Born Again is conspicuously missing from her desk, simply gone, her computer screen blank. All this passes around the office in a quick buzz; the corral takes on a whispering restlessness. After fifteen minutes, she comes out and walks the fastest way back to her desk, no gossip stop, reddened eyes cast down. Everyone looks away as she passes, shunning the diseased animal. At her desk, near mine, she starts shuffling papers with windup toy energy, tossing them in the air, opening and closing her drawers, as if she's scrambling through her bedroom bureau at home, searching for underwear. She crawls under her desk so that only her neat little skirt and the spike heels of her pumps are showing, and starts pulling out shoes and plastic bags and tubes of Christmas wrapping paper, which she always bought like a sucker to help out her Mine's kid. She paws all this out and behind her like a frenzied dog.

"Let me help you," I keep repeating, still typing. I'm working on a rush document. "No thank you," she says, very polite and formal, backing out and sitting back on her heels for a minute and looking right at me with boiling blue eyes. Her face and neck are splotchy with hives. I go over and start helping anyway, picking up odd shoes and sticking them into two big plastic bags until they look jammed and festive.

When the Italian Princess got fired six months ago, she marched out of the office and returned with a box of Perugina chocolates that she passed around with towering grace, shaming all the Mines, who made a big show of studying the chocolate chart and selecting just the right one, never looking her in the eye. This is something of the spirit and style I hope to have if my day comes.

Born Again and I march past the open office where her Mine sits looking out the window dictating intently, *the trust instruments unambiguously express the Settlor's intent to relieve the Trustees of the structures of the "prudent man" rule.* She doesn't look in at him, but walks quickly past, skittering slightly in her heels, the off-kilter rear end of a beaten animal.

A few others rush out to the elevator banks for a whispered commiseration as she leaves, the brave few, one even riding downstairs in the elevator with us and whispering for a few moments in the front lobby, shivering with cold and fear of contamination. Passionate, holiday-bright farewells, *we'll keep in touch, I'll call you soon, good luck, you'll be fine.* On the sidewalk, I give her a quick hug, looking past her shoulder for a cab.

"I'll call you tonight," I say. "Don't worry."

The cab pulls away and the waters close over her head. I go back upstairs, slouching inside the elevator in a rebel teenage pose. Her Mine's tape is sitting in my box, stink bomb through the letter slot. I pick it up and drop it to the floor, kick it once, twice, toward Born Again's empty desk so it ricochets off the wall. Then I retrieve it and rewind it and put on my headphones and start typing.

I know, already, how it will work. I haven't spoken to Perugina since she was fired half a year ago. I've called her a few times and hung up when she's actually answered. I know I'll do the same with Born Again, just to make sure she's all right and hasn't killed herself or disappeared into a cult. We'll have nothing to say to each other now that our only source of commonality has disappeared. I feel guilty about this although it's no one's fault; once all this disappears, there's nothing left, and the conversation will end up making both of us feel worse, especially me, as I'm still here. A new person will take over her desk and I know Born Again will ask me about that in the way of a jilted lover asking about the New One. I already hear the wistfulness in her voice when I tell her, as I will have to, that her Ex-Mine hasn't once asked about her and seems perfectly happy with Ms. Cheap Designer Suit who eats Weight Watchers frozen entrees and drinks diet Coke every day at her desk for lunch and calls me "Hon-Bun."

.   .   .

The similarities between a barnacle and a secretary are strik-
ing. A barnacle lives all its life stuck to the same rock, and then
finally dies. In one of those bizarre twists of nature, a barnacle is
both female and male at the same time. There seems to me a built-
in satisfaction in this arrangement. Except for the occasional office
affair or secret and solitary sex act that no one ever confesses to,
offices tend to be lonely, asexual places, prisons of marked time.
Barnacles are craggy and imperturbable and just blow spit con-
tentedly, unless some large heel happens to crush them. I sit here
quietly blowing spit, painfully monosexual, waiting for an act of
fate to budge me off this rock.

Dublin has started hearing voices coming from the air vents,
one voice in particular that keeps telling her to arm herself with a
machine gun and return to Ireland. Whenever she goes into the
ladies' room, she insists on turning off the fan. No one wants to ask
whether it's because the noise of the fan obscures the voices from
the air vents, or whether another voice is emanating from the fan
that spooks her into not being able to pee. Someone reports the air
vent tragedy-in-the-making to Dragon Lady who, in turn, brings
it to Biggest Mine's attention. What if she comes into the office one
morning with an Uzi and goes crazy under the psychic auspices
of the IRA? No one wants to accompany her out of the building,
let alone home or to a doctor, because they don't want to get
trapped in the elevator with a psycho. Someone calls building
security. Meek, gallant little Jose is the one assigned to escort her
out. He stands at the elevator banks with her, holding her elbow
gently as though she's his sickly aunt from Puerto Rico and he's

taking her home from the hospital. I tell myself I'll call her over the weekend.

Plant Man comes by my desk this afternoon and gives me a few cuttings wrapped in a wet paper towel. He hands them to me across the desk ledge with this delicate look in his eyes as if he's giving me a bouquet of peonies instead of drooping green leaves cut from some end-of-the-world mutant office plant.

"Take these home and put them in a jar of room-temperature water and put it on your windowsill. You'll get roots in a week or two, I promise. Call me if I've lied to you." As he walks away I pick up a pen and scribble *Executive Plant Power,* which is printed on the back of his shirt, in the margin of the agreement I'm typing, in case I never see him again. I transfer it into my address book under *P* and then white it out from the margin of the document, giving it only one thin coat, careless as to whether or not it dries properly before I return the page to the stack. Let Mine be inquisitive enough to hold it up to his desk lamp and play invisible ink with my life.

Too much coffee this afternoon, I dash into the ladies' room and burst into the first stall, heart and bladder exploding, already pulling up my skirt. Not quite locked, the door pushes open and I come upon one of the Almost Thems with her skirt hiked to her waist, peeing standing up, urine splashing here and there. I am certain that a little ricochets on me before I slam the door shut.

I retreat to the very last stall and hunker down to wait. Almost Mine is taking her time at the sink. I wonder if maybe she's waiting for a little litigious rumble. I've seen her pee like a man and she wants to read me my rights. I don't oblige her, but wait until I finally hear the outer door close. You'd think something like this would work in my favor.

Lately, the owner of Cafe Bella Vista around the corner has started giving me free lattes. This usually happens when I go in late on Friday afternoons, escaping from the office and sneaking down the block when Mine is in a meeting. I tell Call Girl I'll be back in a minute and don't explain where I'm going. I leave with a five-dollar bill in my pocket and my sweater on and emerge blinking into the afternoon sunshine and walk with my face lifted up to the sun as though all my things aren't up there, my cursor killing time blinking in the middle of a word in the middle of a document that has to be done before the end of the day. Big closing. I just walk away, leaving a bad marriage. I put lipstick on, one-handed, as I walk, check the bow of my mouth with my finger to make sure I haven't gone outside the line. I order the latte to go, but then I sit down to wait while Bruno makes it, so I can watch.

Cafe Bella Vista has those tiny unstable wrought-iron tables with tiled tops, and spindly wrought-iron chairs with curved backs that make you sit very straight with your chest out like Sophia Loren. I always sit down carefully and cross my legs slowly so I won't lose my balance. Bruno is usually there by himself this late in the afternoon. He's in his fifties, has shiny black hair, probably dyed, and wears a white apron folded in thirds high on his belly as though he's just about to go out for the evening and can't mess up his shirt. He makes the latte with sweeping, unnecessary motions of his arms and gives me way too much foam on top so that it's dense and shiny, like shaving cream; by the time I reach the bottom of the cup, my upper lip is so stiff I have to scrape the sticky dried milk off with my fingernail.

I want Bruno to offer me a job. I'd make perfect cappuccinos with a dusting of cinnamon on top, wear long silk dresses that showed cleavage. We would get married and spend summers with his mother in a villa outside Rome. On my way out the door, he blows me a kiss. "Thank God it's Friday," he says in his Italian accent. I take the latte back to the office. When I get off the elevator, I edge back toward my desk sideways, holding the purple Bella Vista cup down at my side as though it's a live grenade. Back at my desk I keep the lid on and sneak sips, the steam softening the inside of my nose. I think Mine smells it anyway, he looks at me sharply when he passes my desk. I broke the rules and he's jealous. He's given up caffeine.

I'm updating my résumé. Shift-screen On, Shift-screen Off. Now you see it, now you don't. Momentary hope dive-bombs into despair. I fax it out secretly, a hopeful missile, then wait. *Reinvent, rejuvenate, regenerate, rehabilitate, reeducate, reincarnate, reinstate, reparate.* Alt-F1, Thesaurus.

Unless you're friends with someone, you don't talk about where you're going at night after work, whether you're bustling like crazy to get out of there just to sit on the subway and go home, or going out to dinner and a movie with a friend or to a PTA meeting or to commit a sex crime. We are all just glad to be leaving. This, we share. We are glad that this thing, work, is ending, even though a bleak stretch of time alone with no plans or goals or friends may loom before us. Only a small percentage of us are truly as thrilled as we act to be going home. In fact, it is the simple act of liberation, of leaving the prison, that is the joy. Sometimes, standing in the bathroom as we all lean into the mirror, a row of six women, fixing our faces, I want to ask *"Where are we going?"*

.   .   .

Toilet Water has a collection of perfume ads that she tears out
of magazines. I collect them for her without thinking, the way I
still pocket saltine crackers everywhere I go for Little Pregnant
One. Toilet Water has shown me the best way to tear pages out of
thick fashion magazines at the spine. She stores them flat in a
manila envelope, Scotch-taped to seal in freshness. At night, before
she leaves the office on a date, she takes out one of the pages and
rubs the shiny paper over her wrists, up the sides of her neck, on
her ears and across her breasts outside her clothes. She looks up
and down the hall before she does this. She reseals the paper flap
carefully to preserve the scent and replaces the magazine page in
the envelope. She keeps this envelope in her drawer in a file
marked "After Hours." Inside the green Pendaflex file she also
stores a deodorant, body cream in a pump bottle, a miniature
Scope and a plastic palette of mauve eyeshadows. While the lifetime of these perfume pages is not indefinite, they generally retain
enough scent to last until she borrows another magazine from Call
Girl. She keeps a few pages of men's cologne samples from *GQ*
as backup. "Men can't tell the difference," she says. "How do I
smell?" she asks, coming up close and thrusting her breasts toward
my face. I sniff once, twice. "Floral, musk, a hint of paper," I
tell her.

At one minute to five, I race to catch the elevator going down
and recognize Plant Man's hand waving over the magic eye inside
the door, my Merlin. We stand awkwardly braced in opposite corners of the elevator, suddenly self-conscious. His green plastic
watering can is sitting between his feet along with a half-dead

palm, its brown-tipped fronds drooping over his right hand, which holds the stem upright.

"ICU," he says, gesturing down toward it with his head.

"Where's that?"

"My apartment. Kind of a plant sanitorium."

I reach over and pull off one of the brown leaves. "Will this one make it?"

"Maybe. With bed rest and real light."

"Just what I need," I say, and hand him the leaf. He folds it and puts it in his kangaroo apron pouch.

On the ground floor he holds the door open so that I walk out first, then he follows with the plant container tucked under his arm like a body, the head of the palm leading.

"See you," I say, looking back at him once, twice, as I turn the corner.

"Later," he says, and waves.

The end of work on Friday is a black hole. Mine leaves early to go away to his country house. He and his wife make calls back and forth during the afternoon. I hear them from my desk. He reminds her about picking up his golf pants from the cleaners. She reminds him to order a case of wine. He calls out to me to come in and then he hands me a list. I consider ordering a bottle of the $21.99 California chardonnay, "an oaky gem with hints of manure," for myself, but he picks the wine up himself on the way out of the city, he would notice. They travel in separate cars. She usually takes the children. I imagine them passing on the highway as they're talking on their car phones, the children looking up and waving calmly at Daddy, like royalty.

I don't want to go with Mine, but the way it all ends so abruptly on Fridays makes me feel cheated. You wait for this moment to arrive each week like a Priority Mail package, and then when it does arrive, it's empty. Partly it's the waiting, partly the bittersweet truth about something longed for. He never asks what I'm doing for the weekend. He has no idea whether I am now, or ever have been, in love; whether I always eat alone. I think they learn this in law school, not to ask. I leave the office alone, set adrift. Outside everyone is racing for the subway entrances as though they're all going to big fancy parties. I go down into the subway, a gentle pink sexy Friday evening. The subway envelops me in fumes and nine-to-five body smells. I dart for a seat, claim it, avoiding eye contact, appreciate my relaxed melancholy, envision a glass of wine, California chardonnay, $6.99 a bottle.

I've stolen a litigation bag.

A Friday night loose end, a litigation bag was left on a desk near mine, upright and square as an undertaker's bag, with the kind of simple metal fastener that once closed my dollhouse. On my way out, I swing the bag up with one hand, still walking, as though removing luggage from an airport carousel. Who would stop me? Where is "litigation bag" in the building's security manual? There is something sinister and private in the sound of "litigation bag," some relation to enema or douche bag. When Mine calls me on the intercom and tells me he needs one, I feel slightly embarrassed, as if he's requesting a sexual aid. Litigation bags are inexpensive imitation leather, awkward to jam into the overhead compartments of planes. I make plans to use it as a city picnic basket, a plumber's caddy, a secret hamper for my underwear. This theft is probably equivalent to stealing one of the U.S. mail bags you see dropped at the legs of mailboxes like dead gray animals, tethered. About this, too, I will await a confidential e-mail summons. Mine may interrogate me regarding this matter in the next week. In anticipation, I will practice Zen. I will look directly into his eyes, right into their very dark centers, remain attentive and interested, somewhere very far away, perhaps creating a Japanese flower arrangement, establishing the balance of three pussy willow branches in the perfect *shin*. I am quite pleased that, without going to law school, I now own this artifact of authority. My bottle of chardonnay fits nicely inside the bag, rolling gently between my feet with the movement of the subway.

· · ·

Sunday night. I construct an effigy of Mine out of pieces of straw pulled from my broom. I give him a butcher string waist and a button head. I lasso a small shiny black beach stone with string and hang it around his neck. This is his dictating machine. I prop Straw Mine on my altar and let him just stand there like a dunce. I start the paper bag and honey cure suggested by the Spanish coffee-grounds psychic, tear two pieces from a brown shopping bag and write my name and Mine's on two separate pieces and crumple them up. I can't bring myself to submerge them into an almost brand-new jar of expensive clover honey, imagining how I will gag if they end up, like marinated roaches, on my toast one morning. Instead, I place the crumpled bits of paper in front of Straw Mine on my altar where they look like two club feet. The next morning, I sweep the whole thing into a bag and put it out for Monday morning garbage collection.

Lying in the bathtub on Sunday night, I dictate my resignation. I cover my breasts with a washcloth and prop the dictating machine under my chin. I fast-forward the tape to the middle of side A. "Pursuant to the above-referenced matter," Mine is saying. I press Record, interrupting him. "Pursuant to absolutely nothing," I begin, "I hereby tender my resignation." Pause. The tape whispers. "Tender is as tender does," I add. I click off the machine and dip it away from my chest toward the water, circling my wrist in the proper attorney stirring motion, then bring it back to my lips. I clear my throat. "By the time you hear this, I'll be gone. Don't try to find me." I click it off again and stare at the pink, Jell-O-y blobs of my toenails under the water, take a sip of my wine, then press Record again. *"Rock that pony, turn that pony, ride that pony home,"* I chant. When I play back the tape, waves are slapping against the sides of the tub.

... In the event that this Agreement cannot be performed or its obligations fulfilled for any reason beyond the reasonable control of the parties hereto, including but not restricted to, acts of the Government, war, fires, floods, epidemics, quarantine restrictions, strikes, freight embargoes, unusually severe weather, or Acts of God, then such nonperformance or failure to fulfill its obligation shall be deemed ...

MONDAY

MONDAY MORNING, WHILE HE'S STILL STUCK IN EXPRESSWAY traffic, I go into Mine's office and throw my tape into the box with all the others and jumble them together. Returning to my desk, I stare into space for a long time, sip my coffee, then log on to the computer. I whisper my possible future good-byes to Bad Dog who simply scratches the screen near my face and lifts his leg in my direction.

Mine comes down the hall, his briefcase slapping his thigh, his head in the *Wall Street Journal.* He looks tan.

"Bring your pad in," he says, not looking at me. I follow him into his office and take my regular seat. He places the briefcase on his desk and takes off his jacket, folding it so that the silk lining is turned outward. He shakes the jacket gently, midair, as though he's performing a magic trick and tweaks the cuffs one at a time until the sleeves fall perfectly. Draping the jacket over the back of a chair, he sits down, brings his feet to the desk. He dips his hand into the box of tapes and begins idly playing with them, picking up one and then another, upending them like dominos, then knocking them over. I strain to tell which tape is mine. Russian Roulette meets Mission Impossible.

"Let's not waste any time," Mine says, bringing his chair crashing to the floor. I stare down at my steno pad, pencil poised, waiting. In the distance, I can hear Bad Dog barking.

2